GLOBAL TAKEOVER

@ Tipton Saga

Philip Davidson

Imprint: Independently published
ISBN: 9798505057179

Cover and interior layout for this edition by Philip Davidson

Please note this edition is formatted for English spelling, which is slightly different from American spelling.

DEDICATION

To the Earth, hoping it sorts itself out.

CONTENTS

Introduction

Good morning, afternoon, or evening. My name is Philip Davidson and I am a first time author. It may come as a surprise to learn that Global Takeover is the third part of The Tipton Saga. The Tipton line dates from 1810, when the first Tipton twins were born, and they were raised in a Black Country orphanage. The present day Tipton girls only became aware of their strange heritage in 2019 when their wild adventure began. The first part of The Tipton Saga takes place in the early 1800's, the second part in 2019, and Global Takeover in 2020. To find out more about the first two books you can read *'the story so far'* at the end, along with the rationale for releasing Global Takeover first. I don't want to confuse with more and simply urge you to dive in and take up the story in 2020. It may be helpful to explain a little of one character in this fantasy comedy; George William. He was in a position of global power when he was incarcerated in 1810 due to a bout of insanity. During his long incarceration he dreamt up a perfect world empire and for the next two hundred years pitched for another go. By 2019 he was successful and back on earth.

Global Takeover is a fantasy - or is it? Definitely a comedy; hairy at times. Expect the unexpected and enjoy the ride into *Dystopian Comedy*. Welcome to 2020 and Global Takeover.

Memories fade; fade so very fast. Fade to a point where they seem normal; the new normal. The weird decent into the first 2020 lockdown, remember? Were strange things were going on? Of course; individuals were seeding dastardly plans to take-over the Earth! And you are about to discover what these plans are!

2020

The year of vision and clarity, for some...

CHAPTER ONE

1

As the virus floated over from the orient, George William's plans were flung into disarray. Planes stopped flying, businesses locked down. Everything came to a sudden halt. Almost the entire human population stayed indoors; some ordered to do so.

"Ordered to stay indoors! Ordered!" Prince Fredrick commented. "Is that not extraordinary?"

Hubert nodded respectfully. "That does sound extraordinary!"

"This meant George William's newly manufactured robots were forced to lay idle. I should mention that Mr Figgis's design for these robots is very convincing. Mr Figgis is at the top of his game on this. Hard to distinguish between his robots and real human beings."

"Hard to distinguish … extraordinary!"

"These particular robots are the rumour-mongering ones designed to mingle with the general public and propagate George William's vision of a perfect world. They will be operating in bars and clubs. I presume the hope is that the public will think what a bloody good idea his perfect world is, start spreading the news, George William would pop up, and the people would let him get on - with it."

"Extraordinary … very good!"

"No, Hubert, I think it is naïve and will not work. You cannot expect people to allow him to take over the world on the strength of rumours heard in a few bars. Alright millions of bars. In any case, he cannot do it at present, because the world is locked down and nobody is around to listen to his rumour-mongering robots. I am beginning to think George William is not really up to the job. With all these fabulous modern resources available to him, he cannot seem to properly adapt."

Hubert shook his head. "Cannot adapt…extraordinary!"

"Hubert, will you stop saying 'extraordinary'. It is getting very annoying."

"Yes sir, sorry."

"I am becoming worried now because while George William is floundering, his opponent, Mr Zakamonsky, is positively storming ahead. Mr Zakamonsky is seeing dozens of opportunities in this 'lockdown' to further his takeover of the Earth."

"Mr Zakamonsky – I am assuming you will explain who he is later?"

"I will, Hubert. There is a certain urgency to this. It is the reason I have brought you in. This global shutdown is a strange affair. I can see it is more than possible that other people and organisations will see opportunities in this fog to take over the world. I do not want to give them that opportunity."

"Of course you don't, sir."

"I want to concentrate on the three parties I know about and hope one of them takes over before anybody else gets the idea."

"Excellent idea."

"Obviously I know about George William because I am his father. His bloody father that's what I am. There is a certain status in father-hood you know."

Hubert gave a deferential nod. "Yes, sir."

"I know about Mr Zakamonsky, too: horrible, horrible man. Both these men have been planning their takeover of the Earth for a very long time, so they have a head start. There is a third party in the frame, Georgina Tipton."

"Georgina Tipton?"

"Yes. She is George William's great-great-great-granddaughter. An unlikely contender, but I think she may be the one that will prevail."

"So the money is on Georgina Tipton?"

"Hubert, this is not a game. It is the future of the Earth we are dealing with."

"Yes sir, sorry."

"As you know, I have been dead for over two-hundred-and-fifty years, but very soon I shall have the same status as George William: alive and functioning and back on Earth."

"Is it your aim to rule the Earth?" Hubert asked cautiously.

"My aim is to see which way the wind blows, but I do have a certain unshakeable mission to fulfil."

"And you wish me to be at your side and be your supporter?"

"Precisely. We shall use our present status to hover over each of the three parties and determine which way the wind is blowing. We shall start with Mr Zakamonsky."

"Mr Zakamonsky - the one that is currently storming ahead?"

"Yes. Even though I believe Mr Zakamonsky to be a diabolical individual, with a great preponderance to do very terrible things at the drop of a hat, I believe his motives are rather noble."

"Why is that, sir?"

"Hubert, you have to understand that Zakamonsky comes from a place you have never seen. He is Emperor of a sister planet to the Earth; a place not many people know about. So near, yet so far. I've seen it: a kind of reddish place. He has promised his people a better life on Earth; a way to improve themselves. I said 'noble', but should say 'half-noble'; not even that. Zakamonsky is a terrible dictator to his people and I presume he will continue to be a dictator to them on Earth. He will be a dictator to humans, too, if he succeeds."

"So Mr Zakamonsky will be one contender we do not want."

"We may not want him, but may end having him. Zakamonsky has captured one of Mr Figgis's secret robot manufacturing plants. A plant in the Mojave Desert in California."

"What is he going to do with that?"

"Many things, but immediately he is planning to use the robots to capture two Hollywood studios."

"Why does he want to do that?"

"Two reasons: he wants the ability to make alien-friendly films. I have seen the plot for a series of films called The Zaki Family. They are touching accounts of a deformed alien family living on Earth who are always doing good deeds, and they are always getting put down because they are not human. He's given them sweet little faces, and bambi-like eyes. You could not help liking this family and feeling sorry for them. They even have a pet mouse with a cute little nose, the Zaki Mouse, all designed to pull on the heartstrings and before you know, they are *actually* living on Earth."

"I can understand the reasoning behind that strategy, sir. What is the reason for capturing the second Hollywood studio?"

"The second one, yes; very curious indeed. Mr Zakamonsky has come into contact with Georgina Tipton and fallen in love with her. I would more describe it as a raging lust."

"Sounds distasteful!"

"The point is that there is a rumour that Zakamonsky has never had any feelings for anyone, either on Earth or in his own realm. Just Georgina Tipton; she is the first and only one."

"Bit inconvenient isn't it sir? She being on George William's side, so to speak; being his great-great–great-granddaughter and everything. That would mean she is one of your granddaughters, too."

"Yes, hadn't thought of that."

"Does she like the man? Is she fond of him?"

"No!"

"Bad news. Are we planning some kind of rescue mission?"

"No, no, no, Hubert. You are missing the point. We are here to observe which of the three are likely to prevail; possibly a combination. Then we can make our next move. Keep pace with where I'm going."

"Yes, sir. Many apologies for not anticipating your thoughts."

"Apology accepted. The reason Mr Zakamonsky needs the second studio is for Georgina Tipton. As a gift for Georgina, and a way of wooing her. Part of his wooing process."

"Wooing process? I see. Hadn't we better put a stop to that? Who knows where wooing can go? Dangerous stuff wooing. She could even succumb to being wooed by his wooing charms, end up on the wrong side."

"Hubert, if you don't stop interrupting, I shall have to punish you."

"Yes sir, very sorry."

"For these two good reasons, Mr Zakamonsky wants to capture two Hollywood Studios: one in order to make alien friendly films, the other for Georgina Tipton. To fulfil the Hollywood seizure mission, he is using a small commando force of robots from the secret Mojave robot plant; the one he captured from Mr Figgis.

"That is a bit of a tangle isn't it, sir? Mr Zakamonsky using Mr Figgis's robots?"

"Exactly. He cannot know whether Figgis is still in control of them or not. I would love to see the expression on his face of him not knowing this."

"I understand: you would love to see that expression."

"More, I want to see these robots in action. See if they really are able to carry out their mission, see how good Figgis's humanoid robots actually are. The last time Zakamonsky tried replacing humans was in 1961."

"How are these robots going to carry out their mission?"

"We shall have to wait and see because I don't know. What I can tell you is the head of the commando force is a robot called Mr Reynolds. He has sent a film script of The Zaki Family to the chief executive of a certain studio, along with the offer of two billion-dollar investment in the studio."

"Does he have two billion dollars?"

"No; he is a robot! I suppose he could do something with computers to make it look like he has the money but that is not the point. Los Angeles is locked down. The film studios are locked down. No productions are being made; they are haemorrhaging money. An offer of two billion is a substantial carrot; it has worked. The Chief Executive has invited Mr Reynolds to the studio to discuss it. I want to see how Mr Figgis's robots act in the field. They will be meeting in the next few minutes. We shall now hover over the scene and watch."

"Yes, this will be exciting."

"I had better warn you: the robots may act strange."

"Strange? Why is that?"

"They are likely to be an extension of Mr Figgis – brilliant technically, but childish in manner. Just like Figgis. An ingenious mind with the mentality of a child. Come on – let us hover!"

2

It was like the Plague in Los Angeles; locked-down, very few people on the streets: a deserted ghost town. The studio at the other side of Hollywood was locked down. The CEO's secretary, Nancy, arrived on the abandoned lot and, quite spooked, opened a small unit housing the CEO's executive office. A few minutes later, the CEO arrived, went up to his office and settled into his seat. A few minutes after this, Mr Reynolds arrived. He was shown up a short curved stairwell, and into the CEO's office. Mr Reynolds carried a big round box tied with a decorative ribbon; perhaps a cake. He put the box on the floor.

The CEO stood up and offered his hand to the robot. "Sure good to meet you, Mr Reynolds. Let's talk. Please sit down."

Reynolds sat.

"We can absolutely make The Zaki Family for you, and discuss your two billion-dollar investment, too. We can work on the Zaki Family as soon as we are open again."

"Have you read the script?"

"Yes, wonderful stuff. Great humour. Even written out a number of suggestions to bring out the humour further."

"Have you?"

Reynolds abruptly rose up and disabled the CEO with a quick chop and dragged him into a cupboard. He detached him from his trousers, and put them on as his own. Did the same with the CEO's shirt tie jacket and shoes. Next, he scanned the man's head with Figgis's brain-scanning device, and downloaded the information into his memory bank. Then he opened the ribboned box, which contained a replica of the CEO's head. He unscrewed his own head, putting it on the desk, and screwed on the CEO's head. Finally, he sat in the CEO's chair, put his feet up on his desk, and calibrated the CEO's voice. He lifted the phone and called down to his secretary.

"Nancy, a coffin will be arriving," he said.

"A coffin?"

"It will be arriving on the lot. I want to see it."

Through the reception window, she saw a hearse pull up and two men in black coats get out.

Nancy asked cautiously: "Why do you want to see a coffin?"

Reynolds, rapidly assimilating the CEO's manner, became more strident.

"Why, why? Because we are in the movie business! Mr Reynolds wants to show me his coffin and I want to see it. I am looking at Mr Reynolds right now." He was looking at Reynolds's head on the desk. "Mr Reynolds has a coffin to show me; a new take on early James Bond gadgets and I need to see it immediately. Two of Mr Reynolds's associates are outside with the coffin. Let them in, and send them up!"

The two robots, like pall bearers, were waiting outside holding the coffin on their shoulders. Nancy shrugged, unlocked the reception door and gave the robots passes. "The CEO will see your coffin now."

Nancy directed them to the staircase. The robots carried the coffin up the stairs and into the CEO's office, and lowered the coffin onto the floor. "Delivery of one coffin, Mr Reynolds," one of the robots said, standing to attention and saluting.

"Very good, Jenkins. Shut the door an open the coffin."

The door was shut and the coffin opened. Inside, another robot, Officer Cunningham, climbed out and saluted to Mr Reynolds. Reynolds saluted back, but Cunningham's salute was odd as he had no head; the robot's hand simply saluted to an empty patch of air where the head should have been.

"When do I get my head?" Cunningham grumbled from a speaker in his navel.

"I will design you a head tonight. Now stop complaining and stand still while Officer Jenkins screws the Reynolds head onto your body."

Jenkins grabbed the Reynolds head from the desk and screwed it onto Cunningham's body. Reynolds inspected Cunningham, now wearing the Reynolds head. "Don't get ideas that you are really me, Cunningham. Do you understand? You only impersonate me for a few seconds on the way out; that is all. Is that clear?"

"Yes," Cunningham replied grimly from his navel.

"OK men," Reynolds said to the other two, "get the CEO out of the cupboard and shove him in the coffin."

"Is he dead?" a third robot, Officer Meekings, asked.

"He is not dead. Get him back to base before he wakes up. Put him in the pen with the others. Go on, get to it!"

The robots bundled the CEO into the coffin and the lid was shut. Officers Jenkins and Meekings lifted the coffin onto their shoulders and made their way downstairs.

On the way out, Nancy asked Reynolds, "Did our CEO like the coffin?"

"Yes," Officer Cunningham said from his navel. Nancy looked at him oddly.

Meanwhile, upstairs, Mr Reynolds wasted no time in getting the capture of the second studio underway. From his memory bank, he accessed the CEO's relationship with a rival studio, a man called Chuck Nadler, and called him on the phone.

"Chuck. Everything good with you?"

"No, not good: locked down. Haemorrhaging money. What about you?"

"I have had an investor over. He has a particular love of coffins."

"Some kind of kook is he?"

"Nothing like that. He wants to invest two billion dollars in a studio. He is one of these secret stock market wizzes: always picking the right stock, moving it into the next right stock. Made billions: now he wants to invest two billion in a studio."

Chuck Nadler asked cautiously, "What does he want for his two billion investment?"

"Not much. He will let you decide. Simply wants you to make his little comedy film. Vanity project. It would cost five million tops. He wants you to see his coffin too."

"What is with the coffin?"

"He has spent years making it. Thinks it is the twenty-first century answer to the James Bond Aston Martin."

"What does it do?" Chuck Nadler scratched his head, puzzling. "What can it do? Does it fly? Is it a silly flying coffin?"

Reynolds shook his robot head. "Does not do anything. Got a few gizmos inside, that is all. He is very proud of it. All he wants is for you to compliment his work on the coffin."

"Why don't you make his picture and admire his coffin? We could all do with money right now."

"I blew it, Chuck. I did not admire the coffin. He got in a huff and said he would take his money elsewhere; I messed up. Thought you might be interested – he is still around. Do you want to see him?"

"Sure, I'll check him out. He sounds like an idiot."

"When?"

"Give me forty-five minutes to get my office open. I will get Mary in and some security."

“Forty-five minutes?”

“Yes.”

Reynolds put the phone down and pelted downstairs. “Nancy where did those guys with the coffin go?”

“They drove into the desert.”

“I will be back in an hour,” Reynolds said, and raced off in the CEO’s Lamborghini onto the desert road. He caught up with the hearse and screeched out in front, road-blocking them. Jenkins was driving the hearse.

“What is up, Mr Reynolds?”

“I need my head back. Cunningham, give me my head back!”

“I will be without a head again.”

“Just hand it over and get back in the coffin – we have another job to do.”

“The CEO is in the coffin.”

“We will get him out. Dump him in the desert and tie him up.“

Jenkins and Meekings got the CEO out of the coffin. He was still asleep; still in his underwear. They hauled him over to a cactus and sat him up. Jenkins tied him to the cactus. His head slumped down and he started snoring. They left the studio boss in his underwear, head down snoring, and got back in the hearse.

Jenkins raced the hearse raced back to the city. Forty-five minutes later, Mr Reynolds was in the office of Chuck Nadler.

“Mr Reynolds, welcome,” Nadler said. “I am excited to meet you. I want to hear about your picture. Sit down; tell me about it.”

"Do you want to see my coffin?"

"I do! I would like to see your coffin."

Jenkins and Meekings carried the coffin into the office, placing it on the floor.

"Would you like to see inside?"

"I would like to see inside your coffin," Nadler said, slowly. "This is something I would like very much to see."

"Fine," Reynolds said, and gave him a chop. Cunningham jumped out of the coffin and helped bundle Nadler in. He was detached from his shirt, trousers, socks and shoes. For the next three minutes, head screwing, dressing up and brain transfer was carried out. Then, all set, the party left.

"Thanks Mary, the meeting was a success," Nadler – aka Mr Reynolds – said on the way out. "Lock up and go home. We will meet again next week and see what the pandemic situation is then."

Reynolds, now outside on the lot, approached the rest of the unit as they loaded the coffin into the hearse. "Well done, men," he said. "Take this one back to base and pick up the other one on the way."

"You not coming with us, Mr Reynolds?"

"No, I shall stay here and await further orders."

Jenkins drove off in the hearse.

Reynolds wandered over to Nadler's Velocity Blue F-type Jaguar, and calculated the situation. Now that he was CEO of two Hollywood studios, he assumed he would be changing heads and clothes constantly, and fluctuating between the two studios. He needed to know what to do next. To do this, he contacted his superior, Chief Robot Robert.

Chief Robot Robert was a humungous robot based on the island of Cyprus.

"Mission accomplished," Reynolds reported. "What should I do next?"

"Well done, Mr Reynolds." Chief Robot Robert responded. "Stand by for further instructions."

Chief Robot Robert contacted Mr Zakamonsky.

"Mission accomplished, Lord Z. What should Mr Reynolds do next?"

On one of his rare moments of congratulating an underling, Zakamonsky said: "You have done well Chief Robot Robert, but why stop there?"

"I am not understanding, Lord Z?"

"If we can replace two chief executives, we can replace one thousand. I want all key personnel in the Los Angeles film industry replaced by my robots."

"What is the purpose of this, Lord Z?"

"I want the entire film industry under my control for the time I will require change. For now I want all CEO's and Presidents to carry on as normal. Arouse no suspicion: everything normal. Capture them, but carry on as normal."

"I will instruct Mr Reynolds to carry out this new mission. What should Mr Reynolds do if any of the key personnel do not wish to see your coffin?'

Zakamonsky said, "For ones that do not wish to view the coffin, Mr Reynolds should have an ambulance standing by. The 'Zaki Ambulance Service' it should be called. Ha, ha! Reynolds should enter homes by any means, knock out the personnel, and carry them out on a stretcher to the ambulance. The ambulance should deliver them to the holding pen in the Mojave Desert."

"Instruction received, Lord Z."

Zakamonsky continued: "Chief Robot Robert, I have a deep love of coffins; that is my preferred method of transport. Work on the coffin method."

"Yes, Lord Z."

"Now instruct Mr Reynolds to replace all key personnel with my robots."

"Consider it done, Lord Z."

Chief Robot Robert relayed this to Mr Reynolds, and he stepped up to fulfil his massively expanded mission.

Over the next few days had heads of all key personnel fashioned. He ordered up three teams with hearses and coffins to replace key personnel of the Los Angeles film industry. The holding pen at the Mojave base was filling up. Many did not want to see the coffin; for those, the 'Zaki Ambulance' was deployed. Soon, Reynolds saw it was far easier to use the ambulance – no need for stories; quicker and simpler to break into the property and carry them off with the stretcher. There were a lot of hearses and ambulances in Los Angeles that week, hearses and ambulances all over town. When it was over, Mr Reynolds reported to Chief Robot Robert. "Mission accomplished," Mr Reynolds said.

Chief Robot Robert relayed this to Zakamonsky.

Zakamonsky said, "Very good, Chief Robot Robert. Now prepare for a major meeting!"

3

Hubert looked at Prince Fredrick shaking his head, "That was easy for the Zakamonsky character."

"Too easy," Fredrick declared grimly. "No sign of Mr Figgis controlling the robots, either."

"Mr Zakamonsky seems quite a determined chap."

"He is."

"Would people not get suspicious with all these hearses and ambulances?"

Fredrick shrugged. "It is a plague; people would expect ambulances and hearses. Zakamonsky is a clever little bugger. Come on, let us see what this major meeting is about. Come on Hubert, let us hover!"

4

The big robot -Chief Robot Robert- was stationed a long way from Los Angeles, on the island of Cyprus. He was inside a huge, hangar-like warehouse three hundred feet below the British Air Force base of RAF Akrotiri. Close up, Chief Robot Robert was an intimidating sight: two hundred feet tall, with huge muscles and biceps. This was Mr Figgis's fantasy warrior.

Zakamonsky was not up close; he was communicating with Chief Robot Robert from a screen in the Mojave base. Zakamonsky asked:

"Why is the head of our Los Angeles Commando Force called Mr Reynolds? This is not a name I would choose."

"He is named after a pet rabbit," Chief Robot Robert replied. "A pet rabbit with big ears that was owned by our founder, Aloysius Figgis. Sadly, the rabbit died many years ago. Mr Reynolds is a memorial to the rabbit."

"Mr Reynolds is a memorial to a rabbit? A rabbit owned by that little weasel Figgis?"

"I would rather you would not call our esteemed founder, Aloysius Figgis, a weasel."

"Jennings, Cunningham, Meekings? Who are they?"

"School friends of Mr Aloysius Figgis, our esteemed founder."

Zakamonsky asked uneasily: "Is Mr Figgis still in control of the Mojave base? Is he in control of that base, and not me?"

"No, Lord Z. You are in charge of the Mojave base. You are the only master of that base."

"Are you sure about that?"

"Yes, Lord Z, I am sure!"

"Then why is my commando unit named after Mr Figgis's school friends, and his pet rabbit?"

"The system has picked up on an existing list of names for new robots, names suggested by our esteemed founder Aloysius Figgis."

"That pesky Figgis; his fingers are all over the system," Zakamonsky thought to himself. "You are sure Mr Figgis cannot hack into my base, cannot start controlling it without me knowing about it?"

"That is correct, Lord Z. The Mojave base is operated from my left foot. All your commands go direct to my left foot for implementation."

Chief Robot Robert wiggled his left foot. It was a large foot, one hundred and sixty inches long. He shook it.

"My left foot is completely locked away from other parts of the system – nobody can access it but you. Similarly, you cannot access my right leg where the other one hundred and ninety-nine bases are operated from."

Chief Robot Robert began shaking his right leg. "Our founder Aloysius Figgis and Lord K are joint masters of one hundred and ninety-nine bases controlled from my right leg. You cannot access their bases." He jeered a little. "The esteemed Aloysius Figgis and Lord K [George William] have one hundred and ninety-nine bases to your one! One hundred and ninety-nine to your one! Ha, ha, ha!"

Zakamonsky did not rise to the bait.

"In that case, Robert, I need to make the most of my one base and step operations up a level."

Robert stopped shaking his leg. "What are your plans? What level are you taking me to, Lord Z?"

"I want to activate my ancillary robot force. As people begin to return to the streets, I want them deployed on market research duties. They should go out with clipboards and ask the public what they think about aliens; I need to know how the public feel about aliens so I can plan accordingly."

"I like new projects, Lord Z," the chief robot said, getting more enthusiastic. "Where do you want the researchers to carry out their work?"

"In shopping malls. They should carry out their research in shopping malls across California."

"I will organise that, Lord Z."

Zakamonsky addressed Robert on a more serious note: "Despite our Commando Force having ridiculous names, they have succeeded in replacing key personnel in Hollywood with robots under my command. I shall now take this to yet another level."

"What are you suggesting, Lord Z?"

"I want to replace all the world leaders with robots who are under our command."

Robert rubbed his hands together. "This is what I like to hear! The brain- and memory-scanning technology means our robots can slip into their roles without immediate detection. This is an exciting project. Where do we begin?"

Zakamonsky thought for a moment.

"I would like to start by replacing the leaders of China and the United States with robots under my command."

Robert began jumping up and down with excitement, rubbing his hands and pumping his giant muscles. "This is a big challenge, Lord Z, something I like very much. Perhaps first I should replace the President's security personnel with our robots? Then our security guards can replace the President's with little effort. A good idea, yes?"

"Formulate your plans, Robert. Submit them to me tomorrow. I shall leave now."

"Before you go, Lord Z, give me instructions about film and television productions: what productions should I instruct Mr Reynolds to make?"

"For the moment, everything should remain as it is. Soon it will change… change with subtle finesse that populations will not even detect. Then I shall turn it up, ratch up pressure, wear them down; keep wearing them down. Wear them down until they are like putty in my hands. Putty!"

His lust for human domination began to rise in him like a torrent, a volcano of pleasure inside him. He quickly put himself in check; he did not want Robert to see this side of him.

"For the moment, everything will stay as it is," Zakamonsky said calmly. "The television series about the Zaki family will go into production without delay. It will begin as soon as I have determined which studio should make it. I wish to give Georgina Tipton a studio. She should choose her studio soon. Once she has chosen this, we will go into production with the Zaki family. Georgina Tipton needs to make her choice quickly."

Again, another torrent of lust began rising in Zakamonsky, an altogether different torrent: an unfamiliar one he did not understand. He began to go silly and gooey. He did not want Robert to see him like this either, but Robert did.

"I can see you are fond of Georgina Tipton," Chief Robot Robert said.

"How can you tell?"

"You are being influenced by a human, I can see. It is called 'love'. You are in love with

Georgina Tipton. She can influence your decisions."

"She can?"

"This thing called love can have a bearing on men's plans. Be warned!"

"Thank you, Chief Robot. You and me are going to get along well."

There was something of a smile about Chief Robot Robert, and something of a smile about Zakamonsky, too.

5

"What do you think, Hubert?"

"Rather more than I expected, sir – replacing all the world leaders, wewph!"

"Yes, now the world is locked down Mr Zakamonsky is acting fast."

"He has that big robot helping him with romantic tips concerning Georgina Tipton too. Yes, rather more than I expected."

"Next we shall visit George William."

"George William, your son?"

"Yes – there is a certain statues in Father-hood, Hubert. A status that should be respected."

"I will respect your status as father of George William," Hubert said, deferentially.

"Good. That will stand you in good stead. Now, let us hover, and assess my son and his chances of ruling the earth."

CHAPTER TWO

1

In fact it was two weeks later when Fredrick and Hubert began their assessment of George William. They were hovering over the scene.

George William was sitting behind a little desk with a pompous imperial flag placed at one corner. He was thumping his fist up and down on the desk.

"It's been months Figgis! I need to get my mission started. We need to get the rumour-mongering robots out doing their work."

"This pandemic has put a great big gob-stopper to our plans, hasn't it?" Figgis said with a grin.

The desk was outdoors; on the sun terrace of a villa near the summit of a small Greek island in a remote corner of the Aegean Sea.

"George William escaped to this secret hide-way after Mr Zakamonsky laid siege to his fortress in Arizona. He laid siege to it with robots from the Mojave base that he'd captured from George and Figgis," Fredrick explained, hovering unseen over his son.

"Getting a little bit troublesome that Mojave base," Hubert commented.

"Yes, a stupid error that has set my son back a few paces. Now keep quiet while we assess George William's chances of taking over the earth."

"Yes sir," Hubert turned rigid, solemn, and in observing mode.

George William bashed his fist down on the little desk one more time.

"Yes, yes! This pandemic has put a delay to our plans, but are people out of their houses yet? Is anyone in the bars?"

Figgis said. "A few…not many."

"If any people are out of their homes, we should get our rumour-mongering robots out there too; get them lingering in the bars and cafés, spreading rumours. They could join queues at bus stops, too, spreading the word. Making me look good. Come on Figgis, get the robots out doing their work!"

"I could send them into the bars and cafés, but we have the same old problem, don't we?"

"What problem is that Figgis?"

"The opening line. What is their opening line? What is the first thing they say when they meet someone in the bar?"

"Opening line, opening line, yes." George got up and strutted up and down the terrace thinking about this. "How about…'There is a man that will bring peace to the Earth. He is here now. He will bring peace to every nation on Earth…'."

"And who would that man be?"

"Me, of course, you idiot!"

"It would sound like the robots are introducing Jesus back to the Earth."

"Hmmm, yes, you are right; it would sound like that. How should we introduce my perfect plan for the Earth?"

"I don't know – it is your perfect plan; I only do robots. You had better get a move on, though; Mr Zakamonsky has already got his robots out there."

George William was alarmed. "Zakamonsky! What is he doing?"

"Just a moment, I will show you."

"Bloody Zakamonsky. I have been pitching my perfect plan for two hundred years; been accepted. I am back! Then bloody Zakamonsky comes along and everything starts to go belly up! With Zakamonsky around, everything goes to pot!"

"I cannot help that – cannot help things going belly up for you all the time. I think you should see what Mr Zakamonsky is doing."

"Is he getting one up on me?"

Figgis put a screen on the desk for George William to watch. It relayed a CCTV feed from a shopping mall in San Francisco. Zakamonsky had deployed his market research robots in the mall, getting them to ask the public what they thought about his warrior aliens. There were only a few people in the mall, most were wearing face masks.

George William looked at the screen, shaking his head.

"People are returning to the malls, but look what it has come to, Figgis. People muzzled, wearing nose and mouth coverings, petrified of the environment they are living in. Terror-stricken by the virus. That is not the Earth that I shall rule, oh no! It will be far different. Yes, my Earth will be completely different from what we are seeing here today. I have been talking to Albert. We have a plan to eradicate diseases from the Earth. Yes, completely eradicate diseases! That is something we could tell the robots to mention."

"Yes, that might catch on."

"Albert has come up with a tough regime to boost immune systems in humans. It will be impervious to any disease thrown at them. Oh yes, everything will be perfect on my Earth. No need for face masks on my Earth!"

"That is all very well sir, and something we should consider for the opening line, but this is not about people wearing masks. See those men, the ones with the clipboards?" Figgis zoomed in on a little cluster of men with clipboards.

"Oh yes: I believe you call this activity 'market research'. Men with clipboards that stop people in the street and ask them silly, annoying questions – things about different products. I suppose the idea is to sell more of their wares. Is that right?"

"I need to tell you something: those men in the mall are not regular market research people. They are robots. Mr Zakamonsky's robots!"

George was startled. "Zakamonsky! My goodness, Zakamonsky has got market research robots out on the streets? What horrible lies are they telling the public? Zakamonsky is a maniac, Figgis. Unhinged! We have to stop him!"

"The robots are not telling the public anything," Figgis insisted, "it is the other way around. They are asking the public what they think about Mr Z's warrior aliens. Listen in: look!"

The robot was showing a picture of one of Zakamonsky's alien warriors to a woman in the mall. The alien looked highly disagreeable, like a giant slug; mean and tough with an unrelenting stony face: his body slimy with sludge dripping off: threatening eyes; fists. The woman looked on, intrigued. The robot handed her a second picture: a group of them side-by-side with the same mean faces and fists and sludge dripping.

The robot asked, "How would you feel if a group of these men moved into the next house to you? Take a good look at the picture. Would you welcome them? On a scale of one to ten, how much would you welcome them?"

George William smiled. "I have over-estimated Zakamonsky. I do not think we have anything to worry about here. Zakamonsky is not going to win over the public with those kinds of pictures. I will give you a wager they will get a very poor response. Then Zakamonsky will see the results, become disheartened, go away, and leave me alone!"

"Not exactly, sir. However bad the situation may look, it can always be made to look appealing. That is the job of the market research, along with the hearts-and-minds campaign. That is how it works nowadays."

"Is it? Can people really be convinced to live next to these highly unappealing men? I imagine they smell; I bet they will pong the place down. They would have to evacuate the whole street to get rid of the smell. Can people really fall for that in this day and age?"

"I'm not sure, sir. Let's watch and see what happens."

Sure enough, the woman shook her head, indicating 'no' – she would not like to live next to those aliens. Next, the robot asked her what type of alien she would like to live next to, and gave her a flip chart with a multitude of body shapes and faces.

"Please choose the kind of neighbour you would like to live next to. Let your imagination run wild. Choose your ideal alien. Then I shall give you one hundred dollars. Use the flip chart to build your fantasy neighbour; don't be afraid!"

"I see what Mr Z is doing," Figgis grinned. "He wants to build up a catalogue of ideal-looking people to move into the neighbourhoods. He will shape robots to look like them. Then a few weeks later, the alien-warriors will replace them, run amok and take over all the neighbourhoods."

George William said, "Huh, Zakamonsky is not going to get the better of me. Let us blow Zakamonsky's little plan out of the water with a plan of our own."

"What plan is that, sir?"

"Find me someone that does want to live next to those sludge-ridden aliens."

"That might be difficult."

"Just do it, Figgis!"

Figgis searched the cameras. "You are in luck…I have found one."

"This will confuse the life out of Zakamonsky," George William said, laughing. "He will not know which way to turn."

The robot was interviewing a long-haired hippy. "So you would like to live next to this alien?"

The hippy said, "Yes."

The robot pressed the picture of the stony-faced, sludge-ridden alien hard at the face of the hippy. "You are sure you would like to live next to this particular alien?"

"In your eyes he is ugly, but look beyond the outside appearance and you will find a beautiful inner self."

"I shall put that down as a 'yes'. Yes, you would like to live next door to this alien."

"That is right, and I shall tell you why."

"No need; a simple 'yes' is sufficient."

"Do you not want to hear about finding the inner self?"

"No."

The robot terminated the interview and moved on. The hippy stopped him. "Mankind needs to accept aliens with universal love."

"Interview over – push off!"

"My views need to be recorded."

"Look you annoying little squirt … go away!"

"Do not tell me to go away!" The hippy grabbed the robot by the collar. "The world will never change. Not with those attitudes. I demand my views be recorded."

"Atta boy," George William said, cheering him on. "Yes – you demand your views be recorded!"

"Get your hands off me," the robot said, pushing him back and giving him a little chop. Maybe it was too much of a chop because the hippy fainted and fell to the ground.

George William's face fell. "Oh," he said.

It caused a ripple amongst others in the mall; they began to take an interest. One man, some kind of medic, approached the hippy and felt his pulse. "Pulse is normal. We should call a doctor to examine him." A security guard got to the scene. "I will get a doctor," he said. The robots arrived on the scene. "No need," one of the robots smiled, "I have already called for an ambulance. The Zaki Ambulance Service."

"Zaki Ambulance Service? Who are they?"

"The best! He will be in good hands with the Zaki Ambulance Service."

A little while later, two uniformed men from the Zaki Ambulance Services arrived, carrying a coffin. The medic was shocked.

"A coffin? He is not dead. I have felt his pulse – he is not dead. Even if he were dead, he needs to be examined."

The ambulance driver said "You do not understand, buster! This is a multi-purpose coffin: a coffin and a stretcher all in one. It is the virus…new regulations!"

The ambulance men dumped the hippy in the coffin and carried him off.

The little crowd looked on, stunned.

"Damn and blast." George William snarled. "He has got one up on me again! I do not think we have anything to worry about, though. Ambulances with coffins: the public will soon see through that. Thuggish ambulance drivers, huh? Zakamonsky's love of coffins – no – the public will reject him. He does not stand a chance. Even so, he has robots out there; our robots! How did we let that happen?"

Figgis said, "If you remember, we agreed to leave one base open for Georgina. We decided on the Mojave base, in case she wanted to make a feature film in Hollywood."

"It was meant for Georgina, not Zakamonsky; I thought she would be my protégé and I could teach her how to run the world."

Figgis explained: "It was left open for Georgina but Mr Z hacked it. Now it is locked; I cannot get into that base and he cannot get at ours. It is unfortunate but the good news is, we still have one hundred and ninety-nine bases and he only has one. One hundred and ninety-nine to one!" Figgis said, gleefully.

George William grunted. "Right let us get back to work…opening lines for the rumour-mongers." He got up and paced the terrace and practised, muttering to himself, "There is a man that can save you from the virus. He is here right now..."

Meanwhile, Figgis was on his control panel trying to discover more information about Zakamonsky.

"Oh no." Figgis murmured.

George stopped pacing and returned to his desk. "What is it, Figgis?"

Figgis shook his head. "Oh no," he repeated. "Oh no!"

"Come on Figgis, spit it out!"

"Mr Zakamonsky has replaced the President of the United States with a robot."

"He has done what?"

"Replaced the President of the United States with a robot."

“You are joking.”

“I am not joking sir.”

“You know what we must do?”

“No, what?”

“We must replace his President of the United States robot with one of our President of the United States robots.”

“I have not got any President of the United States robots.”

“Well, make one Figgis, dammit! We have been sitting around for months. Now we need to do some work.”

“That will be a lot of work. What do you want me to do? Work on the rumour-mongering robots or work on replacing the President of the United States?”

“Suspend work on the rumour-mongering robots. Concentrate on replacing the President of the United States. Yes, a far better plan. We can get the President to say what the rumour-mongers would have said. We could reach millions instead one or two individuals at bus stops. Think what we can do if we can use the President as a mouthpiece. And others…”

“Others?”

“Let us replace all the world leaders. That is the way to go. We have one hundred and ninety-nine bases to Zakamonsky’s one; we have a clear advantage. Zakamonsky is not going to get one up on me!”

“It is a lot of work, replacing all the world leaders – a tremendous amount.”

“I am sure you will find a way.”

Figgis dug his head into the control panel. Very soon he was shaking his head again. “Oh no,” he said, and repeated, “Oh no. Oh no, oh no! Oh no, no!”

“What is the matter now, Figgis?”

“You are not going to believe this…”

“Tell me what it is.”

“Mr Z has replaced the president of China with one of his robots.”

“How did he do that?”

“He got fifty of his robots from the Mojave base, the one we used to have, to fly to China and do the job. He used an aeroplane to get them there!”

“Dammit! That has put a hole in our advantage – even though we have bases all over the world, he can simply fly his robots to where he wants them. He has got one up on me again! You know what we must do?”

“No, what?”

“We must replace his leader of China with our leader of China. China will have a new leader under our control.”

“That may be difficult.”

“Why is that, Figgis?”

“It will be difficult, very difficult. There will be layers and layers of security.” Figgis was beginning to look very tired. “It is a monumental task. Replacing all the world leaders; it is too much for me to do.”

“Nonsense!” George William retorted, rising up, and commenced pacing the patio; assuming the stance of a world statement on the eve of battle.

"Yes," he said, "this is going to be a monumental battle between me and Zakamonsky, an ongoing global conflict; although I am worried as soon as we replace a world leader, Zakamonsky will try to replace it with one of his. The public will be confused. One week, some of the world leaders will be propagating my vision for the world, the next week they will be propagating Zakamonsky's. Confusing for the public. We will have to find a way to stabilise the situation."

Figgis was not listening. He was concentrating on his control panel, digging out more of Zakamonsky's plans, and became rather excited.

"I have tapped into Mr Zakamonsky's palace. I can only do this once in a while, when everything lines up."

"You have tapped into his palace?"

"Yes - I am viewing his palace inside his realm at this very moment. I can only hold this transmission for a short time. Do you want a look?"

"Rather! I would love to see what Zakamonsky gets up to in his palace. Ho, ho, ho!" George rubbed his hands together and sat down to watch.

Zakamonsky was in the bowels of the palace, two floors below ground. Here, a long line of work tables could be seen, and sitting behind them, a seemingly endless line of scientists working with test tubes and doing experiments. The window-less laboratory hall was shrouded in a red mist, as was everything in this realm. In here, the realm's top scientists worked, working in their hazy, reddish mist. As Zakamonsky walked through the hall, each scientist stopped work and bowed towards him; they praised him and returned to work with their test tubes – working to the whims of their Supreme Commander. Zakamonsky reached a small throne where a wizened old man sat. He looked almost ninety-five per cent human through his slug-like body. Zakamonsky said to him, "You are my Chief Scientist."

"Yes, Supreme Commander, you have graciously bestowed this position on me."

"Chief Scientist, I am pleased to announce liberation of our people has come closer."

"That is very good news, Supreme Commander."

"Very soon our people will be able to live on Earth, as promised. I have been on Earth and will return again soon. I have detected a fatal flaw in humans that will enable our invasion to take place much quicker. All efforts in the scientific community must now be concentrated on the invasion of Earth."

"Yes, Supreme Commander – your will shall be done. I will turn over the entire scientific community to concentrate on the invasion of Earth."

"Wonderful. I shall tell you what the flaw is: there has been an outbreak of a virus on Earth and the response has been heart-warming. Human governments have shut down their industries, ordered people to stay indoors and not to mix. Not to mix, unable to organise! Wonderful!"

"Yes, wonderful," the wizened old chief scientist nodded uncertainly.

“I want my own virus: a virus composed of unearthly materials that Earth scientists will never crack. Half the hall should work on the virus.”

“That will be done, Supreme Commander. Half the hall will be diverted from their present activities to work on your virus full-time.”

“Right now, the other half should work on a complex presentation. I will instruct General Lout to work on one aspect of that presentation.”

“It will be done Supreme Commander.”

“I should be in complete control of my virus, and be able to use it at will. It should contain numerous properties, with some purely for my own entertainment. Commence research on this immediately and standby for further instructions.”

“Yes, Supreme Commander.”

Zakamonsky left the chief with his lust for human domination rising. Zakamonsky’s hands became animated as if moulding something. “Total domination of the entire human race, yes!” he muttered to himself. “They will be like putty in my hands.” Zakamonsky walked down the lines of scientists who were now fully engaged with their test tubes, and began foaming at his mouth, his hands becoming even more animated in his moulding movements. “Putty, putty, putty! Humans: putty – putty in my hands! Complete control of humans! Humans, putty, putty, putty, putty!”

The feed faded out and Figgis’s little screen turned to black. Figgis looked at George William and George William looked at Figgis. Both were shocked.

Finally Figgis said: “Bit much, isn’t it? Total control and domination of the human race! That is a big one!”

“I told you he was a maniac. He is a maniac that is out of control.”

“Yes, sir, I see what you mean. The man is a an out-of-control maniac. Him thinking of humans as putty – it is not right.”

“So, what are you going to do about it?”

“Me? I don’t know; not the faintest idea what to do.”

“Then I shall tell you what we are going to do: you are going to track every stage of the development of this virus. Once you have done that, you are going to come up with an antidote.”

“That is a lot of work, sir. Not sure I can manage it all.”

“Figgis, why don’t you do as you are told for once? The future of the entire human race is under threat. So, get to work!”

“Yes, all right, sir.”

Figgis was looking tired; the extra brain that George William had inserted into his skull was sprouting out from his head and looked like an old withered and scaly sausage.

“It is an enormous workload I have now, sir. Doing the rumour-mongering robots, replacing the President of the United States and all other leaders, now tracking composition of an alien virus: a lot of extra work!”

“Listen, Figgis, I shall explain what this new development means: if you track this virus and do the antidote it will mean we can save the world from Zakamonsky's virus. This is very important – we can save humanity and I can become an international hero, which will stand me in good stead when it comes to me ruling the Earth."

"You, a hero? What about me?"

"OK, Figgis, you can be a hero, too: a little hero somewhere below me. Will that make you happy?"

"I suppose so," Figgis said, grimly. "There are a lot of new things for me to do: a lot more work. What are the priorities?

"Priorities, priorities, yes: we want to do them all! Replacing world leaders and tracking the virus should be our number one, joint-top priorities."

"There have been a lot of changes here in the last thirty minutes: suspending the rumour-mongering programme; replacing the President of the United States; replacing all world leaders; now combating Mr Z's infection programme and becoming international heroes. Lot of changes!"

"Yes, there have been a lot of changes in the last few minutes," George rose up, strutting around the terrace. "When you are a world leader like I am, Figgis, you have to respond rapidly to changing circumstances. I have acted quickly and decisively to the threats posed by Zakamonsky, and charted the way forward. This, I have done in record-breaking time. We are solidly on the road ahead now. One thing I can say as a two thousand-dollar fact and it is this: Zakamonsky will not get one up on me!"

"Let's hope not."

George went off in search of a rare bottle of whiskey he had stashed.

2

Fredrick said to Hubert: “What do you think? How would you rate George William’s chances?”

Hubert was a little overwhelmed. “Yes, he too is a bit more than I expected. To be honest, he seems to be reacting to Mr Zakamonsky rather than taking the lead himself.”

“Exactly what I am thinking!”

“And that little chap, Mr Figgis is getting a tad over-worked.”

“Yes. Now let us take a look at the third contender, Georgina Tipton.”

“Georgina Tipton: the one you think may prevail?”

“I do think that, yes I do. I do believe Georgina Tipton could be the one that takes the lead. She is not very far away; just the other side of this villa. George William and Figgis have this side of the villa, Georgina and her party have the other side.”

“Not far to go.”

“No: even though they occupy the same villa, they rarely meet. Both sides of the house are heavily engaged with their own projects. Georgina is obsessed with a stone.”

“Is she? Why is Georgina Tipton obsessed with a stone?”

“Come on Hubert, you shall see. Let us hover over to the other side and have a look.”

CHAPTER THREE

1

Georgina and her entourage were on the south side of the villa enjoying the afternoon sun on their south terrace. Their south terrace had a different outlook from George William's north terrace. Two-thousand feet below them was the ink-blue Aegean Sea. A rocky dirt track descended three miles from the villa down a to a small harbour where the island's fishing boat was anchored. From the terrace, one could see several other small islands, some shrouded in mist. This was a isolated, unvisited part of the Aegean and the distant islands were all uninhabited. Their little island was largely uninhabited too; uninhabited apart from Georgina's party, George William's party, and a strange monastery a mile up the hill. The monks of this strange monastery (a mile up the hill) were the only permanent residents of the island.

Georgina was crouched behind a low glass table on the terrace; concentrating on a beautiful shining jewel. It's powerful golden ray bathed over her body; and she was encouraging it. More than that. She was like some super-witch doing wafting movements, willing the stone. Willing it on. Wafting up from the stone with her hands and willing the it to tether with her.

"Come to me. Come to me, baby! Come to Mama!" she whispered, wafting, her tones getting louder: "Come to Mama baby, yes! Yeah baby! Come to me. You can do it, come to Mama! Come to Mama now! Nothing to worry about. Power up! Power up baby, ignite! Let's do this – yes, let us rock and roll…."

Hubert said, "My word, you are right: Georgina Tipton is obsessed with a stone!"

"I did tell you; I know a little about this stone. This is priority information – you must keep this to yourself. Will you agree to do this and not tell anyone else?"

"I will agree to do that," Hubert said with an affirmative nod.

"That stone was given to my great-grandfather in the Bavarian Forest in 1685."

"Was it?"

"Yes. A strange man from Greece gave that stone to my great-grandfather. In the heart of Bavarian Forest. In the year of 1685. That strange man went on to prophesize,

'*The one who understands this stone is entitled to rule the Earth'*.

My great-grandfather thanked him and took the stone back to his palace in the north.

Well, a rumour got out about those words *'the one who understands this stone is entitled to rule the Earth'*. Obviously, with such a claim, it intrigued my family, and everyone and their dog turned up at our palace; even distant relatives. They all wanted a go at understanding the stone. Some, not even direct family members, petitioned my great-grandfather to take a look at the stone. They gave speeches as to why they saw themselves as particularly suitable to rule the Earth. It was unseemly. This frenzy was over in a few weeks, as nobody could understand the stone; yet there was something strange and lucky about the stone, and it became like a talisman and joined the family's collection of most precious jewels. After my family took over in Britain, it found its way into one of our imperial crowns. Most of the jewels in the crowns had some kind of story, but this stone was shrouded in mystery. All that was known was what the strange man from Greece had said about 'understanding' the stone. Everyone had long since forgotten about that man and what he had said, and it was only ever told to direct heirs: firstborn sons only. My father told it to me and I told it to George William. The legend was handed down father to son."

"Oh, I see," Hubert said, with some shock.

"What do you see, Hubert?"

"You never got to rule. You died before your father died. George William inherited. You never became king."

Fredrick was silent.

"You must have been mortified. The man who never became king. Are you trying to make up now? Are you planning to rule the Earth?"

"Hubert, will you shut up. I have to told you our mission is to see which way the wind is blowing, assess each of the three parties. Now let me get on with my story about the stone."

"Yes sir, sorry."

"One day my father had a bad experience with the jewel and had it coated with a material to blunt its radiance. He never explained what that bad experience was, yet it seemed as though the stone had some dark side. Apart from that, I am certain he never understood the stone. I did not understand the stone either; nobody understood the stone until George Tipton came along. In 1818, George Tipton began to 'understand' the stone. Well, no, he didn't," Fredrick said, shaking his head. "George Tipton, the stupid out-of-wedlock son of George William. A simple lad, and thick in the head too. He did understand the stone a little, but never went on to rule the Earth; never understood the 'ruling the Earth' aspect of the stone. Stupid lad! Nobody else understood the stone either, until two hundred years later when George Tipton's great-great-great-granddaughter came along; Georgina Tipton. She really understood the stone."

"How do you know that, sir?"

"She said, 'I understand the stone.'"

"Where was she when she said that?"

"Inside the Tower of London; that is where the stone was kept. She was visiting The Tower with Charlotte Tipton. The two girls came into the jewel room where the Crown jewels were held. They were housed behind a bulletproof glass cabinet. She saw the stone inside the cabinet and said to Charlotte, 'I understand that stone'."

"She said, 'I understand that stone'?"

"Yes, those exact words: 'I understand that stone.' That is how I know she really did understand the stone; nobody has ever said those words before. Obviously, she understood the stone."

"Hmmm, I see." Hubert said, dubiously. "What happened next?"

"Georgina needed to get the stone out of The Tower so she could begin her work with it. She harangued George William to get it for her. George William asked Figgis to come up with a plan and he did. Mr Figgis came up with the idea of agitating molecules in everything needed to remove stone from The Tower. After the molecules were slowed down, they would become dematerialised. He had a dematerialisation gun to do this job. It took density measurements for all components needed for the removal. George William recruited a bank robber, Tobias Squires, to do the job. Density measurements were taken to all parts of his body and he was dematerialised. He was not very keen about that. Everything was dematerialised to do the job, including the dematerialisation gun."

"Did it work? Did they remove the stone?"

"Yes, it was removed and replaced by a fake stone."

"What happened next?"

"This is the tricky bit – it went slightly wrong."

"Oh."

"The gun was put into reverse. The molecules were agitated into returning everything as normal. The stone did not exactly rematerialise as normal. Nor did Squires; only his fingers materialised. He has been wanting to strangle Figgis ever since."

"Tobias Squires just has a pair of fingers? No body?"

“That is right.”
“What happened to the stone?”
“That was worse: once the coating my father put on it was removed, it turned into a horrendous blood-red stone. It went into Mr Zakamonsky’s realm. Horrible it was. Zakamonsky captured them – Georgina, Charlotte and Squires – he captured the three of them and locked them up on an English health farm.”
“An English health farm – is that where Zakamonsky met Georgina?”
“Yes: they managed to escape the health farm by pointing the dematerialisation gun at the stone. Squires still had the gun on him. It released the stone from the red realm back to its original Earth realm. It looked like the original stone, had the golden rays, but they had lost their power.”
“So, it looks like the original but with no power...”
“Yes. Now you can see why she is desperate to get the power back into the stone. So she can resume her work with it. Now, if you will shut up and stop asking questions we shall see if she can get power back into the stone. Let us watch...”

2

Georgina was getting agitated, the wafting of her hands intensifying, "Come on baby," she coaxed. "Power up! Come on, do it! Just do it!"

Charlotte shook her head. "That is not going to help."

"We have to do something."

"No we don't. The stone has brought us nothing but bad luck. We should abandon it now. It is nothing but trouble."

"Are you mad? All the secrets of the Earth are contained in that stone. The way the Earth should be operated is revealed with this stone!"

"Is it? You can tell all that from the stone?"

"Yes, it has everything; it is the most amazing stone that has ever existed! It will give us the wisdom to rule the Earth. I understand this stone; I think I am the only one that understands the stone. We have to get it back to normal. Squires. Squires!"

Squires was further down the terrace grumbling to himself, flexing his fingers and threatening to strangle Figgis.

"Yes ma'am, what is it?"

A pair of fingers wandered over.

"I want you to tell me about the dematerialisation gun."

"What do you want to know?"

"Do you still have it with you?"

"Yes, I still have it. It is in my pocket."

"The dematerialisation gun is itself dematerialised?"

"Yes. Everything was dematerialised. Mr Figgis dematerialised everything needed to do the job. It was horrible."

"Can you feel the gun? Can you touch the gun for me?"

"Very well, ma'am."

The fingers of his left hand came to rest about midway down where his body would have been.

"Are you touching the gun now? Are you feeling it?"

"I can feel the gun with the palm of my hand. Not with my fingers; I cannot feel the gun with my fingers. My fingers and the rest of my body are in two different places. It is abominable! I am a big beefy fella; I need to get out. I need to get out!" His stubby fingers moved to his chest in a pulling motion as if he was trying to pull his body out. "I need to get out!!"

"Calm down, Squires! We will try and find a way to get you out. Why don't you use the dematerialisation gun to get yourself back? Put the gun into reverse."

"No, no! It is unstable. Mr Figgis said he got dematerialisation by slowing down the molecules. To re-materialise, the gun would be put in reverse to speed up the molecules but it does not happen like that. Look at the stone. The molecules speed up and go wild…I could end up in a much worse place. The gun is unstable. Quite frankly, I would like to get back to my old situation in Hatton Garden."

"Hatton Garden? Nonsense! Your future is here with us. It is a fabulous future: you shall be head of security for my entire empire. Have patience Squires. Now get your hands back on that gun."

"Yes, ma'am."

"I want you to tell me how you would use the gun."

"First, I would point it at the object and take its density measurements. I wait two seconds, pull the trigger, and the object disappears."

"I want you to demonstrate how you would do this. Pick up the gun and point it at the stone."

Squires's palms wiggled the gun out of his pocket, and he moved closer to the stone. He pointed the gun at the stone, his two sets of fingers acting as a gunsight.

Charlotte suddenly cottoned on to what was happening. "You are trying to use the gun on the stone, aren't you?"

"Why not?"

"Why not? Why not!" Charlotte was going hysterical. "Firstly, because Figgis's molecule agitation processes are thoroughly unreliable; Mr Squires has just said so. More importantly, Albert meticulously analysed both the stone and Mr Figgis's molecule agitation process, and discovered the stone could enter any of at least twelve different realms simply by having its molecules agitated. We have already been caught in one realm; it was horrible. It is a lottery which realm we could end up in. We cannot risk it!"

Georgina was thoughtful. "Yes, you are right. Squires, stand down the gun."

Squires returned the gun to his pocket.

Georgina said, “As I remember, we left Albert working to ensure the stone ended up in the Earth realm – in the Earth realm on full power. I wonder if he has finished his studies? Where is he?”

“He has disappeared.”

“He must be somewhere.”

“Gramps has hidden him somewhere on the island.”

“Why?”

“I suppose he does not want us using him – he wants exclusive use of Albert.”

Georgina said, “Let us look for Albert. We should search the island for him. We could get the monks from the monastery to help us.”

“Those monks are weird.”

“You think they are weird?”

“Yes!”

“I don’t think they are weird, but so what? They seem to like us and I bet they could find Albert in no time. They must know every little bit of this island.”

Charlotte nodded reluctantly. “All right, we will set up a search party to look for Albert with the weird monks.”

Squires spoke: “I have a better idea.”

Georgina looked at him. “What is that?”

“I will go around to Mr George William and ask him where he put Albert. I shall walk out of this garden, around the house and into his garden. I shall say to him: ‘With great respect, your majesty, but you are a despicable scoundrel! I do not appreciate you having me dematerialised and I shall beat you to a pulp until you tell me where you have put Albert.' Then I will go around his back and apply pressure with my fingers on his jaw, and keep increasing pressure until he tells me."

Georgina shook her head. "No, I do not think you should carry out that operation on Gramps."

Charlotte said, "Why not? Sounds a reasonable plan to me."

"It is not the right time."

"Why is that?"

"Mr Zakamonsky is coming."

"What do you mean?"

"Mr Zakamonsky is coming to see me in the next forty-five minutes."

"You are not making any sense."

"How else can I explain it? Mr Z is coming to see me in the next forty-five minutes."

"He is coming here?"

"I suppose so, yes."

"How does he know where we are? Nobody knows where we are. It is secret. How does he know?"

"I do not know how he knows. Why are you asking all these questions? All I know is that Mr Z says he is coming to see me in the next forty-five minutes."

"How do you know that?"

"He texted me."

Charlotte was flabbergasted. "He texted you? Mr Zakamonsky uses texts?"

"Yes, why not? Everyone else uses texts!"

Charlotte was stunned. "How long has this been going on?"

"A few weeks. He has been flirting with me. Now you can see why I did not want Squires to go around and see Gramps. If Gramps knew Mr Zakamonsky was flirting with me and coming here, he would go bananas."

Charlotte was struggling to process all this. "Mr Zakamonsky uses texts, has been flirting with you and is coming here in forty-five minutes?"

Georgina looked at her in a simple way and said: "yes."

3

Charlotte was laying out a tea set on the terrace; a fine tea set she had found in the villa. She did not know how Mr Zakamonsky would arrive. She did not understand any of it, but did realise Mr Zakamonsky was an important person and needed a good tea set.

Toby Squires wandered over Georgina, flexing his fingers. "If you need me to restrain Mr Zakamonsky with my fingers, just give the signal, ma'am."

"I will give the signal, Squires."

Charlotte asked in a little bit of a panic, "Has he sent another text? Does he say how he will be arriving?"

"He has not sent another text. I don't know any more than you. Relax, it will be fine."

Georgina was a bit off-guard. She had hoped to power up the stone before he arrived, meet him on her own terms. This had not happened. She put the stone back into its velvet purse for safekeeping.

A little while later a trumpet sounded; and Mr Zakamonsky arrived; appearing at the far end of the patio, all dashing in a black cape. He was blowing the trumpet triumphantly, announcing his arrival. Georgina flipped her eyes.

"Always the showman. What do you want?"

"I want you, Georgina!"

He started blowing his trumpet again advancing on her. As he reached, she began bashing him with a fly swat.

"Get off me, you dirty beast!" she said, bashing him.

"That is good! Keep doing it! I really like you, Georgina."

Georgina flipped her eyes and gave him a good, hard whack. He loved it, and said: "I am a dirty beast. Maybe you are a dirty beast, too!"

"I am certainly not a dirty beast, Mr Zakamonsky, and that attitude is not going to win you any favours."

Zakamonsky backed off. "What would win you over?" he said, with unexpected humbleness.

"Nothing – go away!"

"How about a gift?"

"No!"

Charlotte said, "That is a bit harsh, sis. Let us see what the gift is first."

"OK: what is your gift, Mr Zakamonsky?"

"I think you would like to make a feature film."

"Go on…"

"I can give you your own Hollywood studio to make a film; a studio you can be completely in charge of."

"How are you going to do that?"

"I have taken over Hollywood. Every studio in Hollywood is now under my command."

Georgina scoffed, "Why not give me all the studios?"

Zakamonsky paused for a moment. "Very well, I shall give you every studio in Hollywood – apart from one."

Georgina was taken aback. "You would do that?"

"Yes."

"What do you want in return?"

"Nothing, it is a gift. Nothing required in return."

Charlottes ears pricked up. "I think we should consider this, sis."

Georgina thought about it for a moment. "It is a generous offer, Mr Zakamonsky. Let us think about it in peace. Leave us now and I shall discuss it with Charlotte."

"Very well, my dear, I shall return in an hour to hear your answer."

Zakamonsky walked back down the terrace, through the garden and disappeared into the fields.

Charlotte said, "This is a very good offer, sis. Three months ago we were just ordinary girls living in suburban Pittsburgh. We have got this far – much further than we could possibly have dreamt of three months ago. Because of what has happened, we have thought of so many ideas of how the world should be. Now we have been offered half of the world's television and film facilities. It is incredible. Let's forget about the stone; it has brought us nothing but trouble."

Georgina got up and paced the terrace, thinking about this, and returned a couple of minutes later.

"No!" Georgina said. "We must get the stone restored before Mr Zakamonsky returns. The full glorious power of Earth is contained in that stone. We must restore it; restore it before Mr Zakamonsky comes back. Squires, get the gun out of your pocket." Georgina took the stone from the velvet purse and placed it on the glass table. "Squires, point the gun at the stone!"

"No!" Charlotte said. "Remember what Albert said!"

Squires pointed the gun at close range to the stone, using his fingers as a gunsight. "Are you sure about this, ma'am?"

"Yes. We have to move forward and take that chance."

"Are you absolutely certain about it?"

"Yes!"

"You are not having second thoughts? Don't you want to think about it a little bit more?"

"No: get on with it, Squires, pull the trigger!"

With great reluctance, Squires gritted his invisible teeth and pulled the trigger.

The stone turned an ominous evil green.

CHAPTER FOUR

1

Slowly but surely the stone became green. The sumptuous golden yellow of the Earth realm did not return on full power. Not the glorious sunshine realm of Earth, no.

Squires groaned. "Here we go again."

Like some horrible dream, everything descended into dark, murky greens. Charlotte and Georgina descended into goblin greens, their veins protruding big and unsightly, like roots: first their arms, then their legs. Soon their skin became darker and scaly: dark crocodile green. Their muscles began choking, their breathing labouring. Squires's fingers turned dark mosquito-green. The sky became like a dark green night, then it was not sky at all. Everything blurred and all they could see was the terrace. From the cracks in the terrace, vipers began to rise: green, wriggly vipers. They wriggled out of the cracks, dozens of them.

"I told you we should not mess with the stone," Charlotte said, choking.

"We had to try."

"How are we going to get out of this? We are about to be eaten alive by snakes. What are we going to do?"

Most of the snakes were a few feet away, wriggling slowly, but more were rising out of the cracks, and bit by bit they were being surrounded.

"Perhaps we could use the dematerialisation gun again. Last time it neutralised the stone. We could try."

"Yes we could," Georgina said slowly. "Mr Squires, point the gun at the stone and activate."

"Yes ma'am," Squires said.

The stone stood out, powerfully visible on the glass table, pumping out it's bright, luminous green. Squires prepared to activate the gun.

"No! Do not do it," a voice came.

They all spun to where the voice was coming from. A few yards down the terrace, a whispery figure in a thin, white flowing dress was saying this. Her clothing was torn.

The woman said, "However scary this realm may be, it is still part of the Earth realm; has Earth creatures. The next realm in the cycle will be too hard for you to understand. This gun you have will not neutralise the stone; it will transport you to a deeply alien zone that you will find hard to survive."

Georgina asked, "Who are you?"

"I am your mother – your great-great-great-grandmother. I am the mother of the Tipton family. I am the mother of George and Charles Tipton."

"You are Nefeli? Princess Nefeli?"

"Yes!" There was a tear in her eye. "I finally meet you. You are the one: the one we have been waiting for!"

Georgina was awestruck. A tear welled in her eye, too. "Mother! You are my mother? My ancient mother?"

"Yes! I am here to help, but my power is weak, I cannot stay long."

"What should we do now?"

"There is an antidote to the stone. Like a dock leaf to a nettle, the stone also has a cure: another stone, a little white stone – a beautiful, white stone. Every time you have a misfortune with this stone, the white stone can return you to safety. It cannot return power to the stone, simply neutralise it, but will return you to safety."

"Where is this stone?"

"I gave it to George Tipton. That was in…in 1850. George Tipton realised the power of the stone, but he was a little dumb. We thought George Tipton would be the one, but he was not. You are the one! It has taken all this time, but you are the one. It is overwhelming to see you."

Nefeli began to cry tears of joy.

"Mother, where is this stone?"

"Just hours before George was assassinated, the stone was put in a trunk; a trunk that Charles Tipton brought to America."

"It is inside the trunk?"

"Yes!"

For nearly one hundred and seventy years many generations of the Tipton family had lived in fear of 'the trunk'. The original Charles Tipton had it locked in a Philadelphia vault following his escape from England in December 1850. When it was finally released, and delivered to the Tipton house in Pennsylvania Heights, all hell broke loose. George William and Figgis suddenly appeared, and whisked the two girls off to George William's fortress in Arizona. That was the start of this whole crazy adventure for the girls; it was just over three months ago.

"Mama, the trunk is in Gramps's fortress in Arizona, seven-thousand miles away."

"I have told you about the antidote. Sometime, somehow you must acquire it. For your protection, you should have it in your possession."

Charlotte said, "That time should be now! We need to get around to the other side of the house and tell Gramps about this. We need to do this now!" She was watching the vipers get ever closer.

Nefeli said, "You should not be frightened of these creatures, for they are part of the Earth realm." She turned to Georgina with a longing; an overwhelming heartfelt look of gratitude and relief. "You are the one! You have things to learn. If you are to bring peace to the Earth, you must lead all the creatures within it. You must make peace with each creature of the Earth, for you are their queen. Be a queen to them all with both regal-ness and humbleness."

"Mama, you have faith in me."

"I do, I do! It is the privilege of my existence to see this," she began to sob tears of joy. "My power is weak; I cannot stay long. I will help where I can. I am going…" she began to fade and disappeared entirely.

Georgina was awestruck; her ancient mother, gone. The vipers were closing in; the freakish, green world of the Trimeresurus vipers. Georgina stood her ground. A bigger one, a large long viper with red eyes, began to climb the table. He wriggled his way up, and curled his body around the luminous green stone. His head became upright. His thin, muscular body uncurled and raised up to confront Georgina.

"Are you friend or enemy?" the viper asked this with a husky rasp.

"Friend."

"Why are you here?"

"To make peace with you."

"Peace?" The viper looked at her blankly, baffled.

Georgina asked: "Why cause so much pain – release venom on other creatures? Why do you do it?"

The viper looked even more baffled: "To eat. To protect our families."

"For what purpose?"

"To survive. To continue existing. What other purpose is there?"

"I will help you find your purpose."

"Why?"

"Because I am your Queen!"

"I am the King in these parts," the viper rasped defiantly. "You come here to take over my kingdom. You must be eliminated! That is the purpose of my venom!" He raised his tongue, preparing to snap into Georgina and destroy her with his venom.

Charlotte grabbed Georgina, pulling her away. "Come on, sis," she said, "we are going to find Gramps."

Georgina shook loose. "No! I shall make peace with this creature."

The viper advanced on Georgina.

Then a trumpet sounded.

Lo and behold Zakamonsky was at the other end of the terrace.

"Dear oh me! What have you done?" He came striding towards them, reached the table and withdrew a shining white stone from his cloak. He aimed it at the stone, and everything returned to normal. The stone resumed its yellow, golden appearance, still without power.

Charlotte was relieved. "Wow, thanks Mr Zakamonsky. You are a star!"

Zakamonsky nodded to her.

"You have a white stone?" Georgina asked. "Is it the antidote?"

"Of course! All parts of the stone come with the white stone; it is an essential piece of the package. Unfortunately, your part of the package became discombobulated long ago. Now Mr Figgis seems to have messed up your part of the stone too. It has no power at all!" Zakamonsky chuckled at this statement.

"Can you get the power back into my part of the stone?"

Zakamonsky stroked his chin thoughtfully. "It is not for me to do this. You must do it. If you can achieve this, we can be equal partners."

"I see."

Zakamonsky said: "You must realise I am not exactly an alien. Nor is my planet. We are kind of part of the Earth realm; the fallen sister if you like. My people know they are fallen. They want to better themselves – become more like humans. In reality, they are better than humans; they surpass humans. This is why we want to join with you. So we can regain to where we should be. We are of benefit to you. We can rebuild this planet, which you humans have ruined. You humans have succeeded in sullying this beautiful planet, and we shall rebuild it."

Charlotte nodded. "You talk sense, Mr Zakamonsky."

Zakamonsky nodded curtly at her. "I am doing this for the successful future of the Earth."

Charlotte said, "You are a thoughtful, kind man Mr Zakamonsky."

Zakamonsky nodded curtly.

"I feel a little nervous joining up with you, Mr Zakamonsky," Georgina said.

"Let me show you the gift I will give you."

"What gift?"

"The Hollywood studios! I will show you around. No obligation."

Georgina considered this for a few moments. "OK," she said.

A day and a half later, they were in Los Angeles.

2

"This is fantastic, sis. We are being offered huge studios, some with forty gigantic stages. All for us! It is unbelievable!"

They were in a Cadillac limousine driving through the tall, palm-tree-lined avenues of Beverly Hills. The girls and Squires were in the back, while Zakamonsky and Mr Reynolds were in the front. Mr Reynolds was driving.

"Yes, unbelievable," Georgina said.

"Unbelievable but true," Zakamonsky remarked. "The art of acquiring what you need, or do not need, is very simple. Simply use the easiest method available; in this case, robots. Get robots to do it for you! Isn't that right Reynolds?"

"Yes, Lord Z," the robot said, respectfully.

Mr Reynolds had shown them studio after studio; large studios, small studios, little animation studios. Dozens of studios; Mr Reynolds had acquired them all. An RV was following on behind, and before each new studio tour, Mr Reynolds would nip into the RV and, like Superman, change into the CEO outfit of that particular studio. Everywhere they went, they were treated like royalty.

"Anything taken your fancy? Has something tickled your imagination, my dear?"

Georgina was trying to look unconcerned, but was actually raging with temptation for the films she could make. Zakamonsky could see this, but bided his time. Fortunately, a distraction arose: Squires's fingers began twitching as they drove past several massively expensive jewellery stores in the Beverly Hills boulevard.

"Control yourself, Mr Squires!" Georgina snapped.

"Yes, ma'am."

Properly composed, Georgina said: "Where are we off to next, Mr Zakamonsky?"

"I am glad you asked that, my dear. We are heading to an experimental cinema – the most advanced of its kind in the world!"

A few minutes later, they arrived at this 'experimental' cinema. It was small: only twenty-five seats; deep plush, and futuristic.

"This is the most advanced virtual reality experience in the world," Zakamonsky said proudly. "How do you fancy getting your hands on this one?"

Georgina looked at him poignantly. "OK Mr Zakamonsky, what is the deal? What do you want back in return?"

Zakamonsky was thoughtful. "I will level with you. I want you to join with me: join willingly. You should not do this under duress."

"Very thoughtful of you."

"Sounds reasonable, sis," Charlotte said.

"I want to treat you to heights you could barely imagine."

"Is that right?"

Zakamonsky nodded. "Did you bring your stone?"

"I always bring the stone; everywhere, I bring the stone!"

She took it out of her bag and looked at it, forlornly.

In a moment of lightning ruthlessness, Zakamonsky withdrew his stone – his blood-red stone – and shone it into her stone, which turned blood-red, too. Georgina's face dropped in shock.

Squires groaned. "Oh boy…here we go again!"

The girls' and Squires's fingers turned a reddish colour, and their bodies locked for a while in a kind of rigor mortis. The whole of the cinema turned a misty red.

"You have tricked us, Mr Zakamonsky! I am not impressed! This will not win me over. Reverse this immediately!"

"Not tricked, my dear. Simply showing things from my perspective. You will be impressed. I wish to show you my plan in all its glory."

"Is that your two hundred year plan for the Earth?"

"It is. I will take you through every stage of the plan. You will experience how the Earth and humans will evolve over the next two hundred years, under my rule. My creative team have prepared this assimilation, and I am pleased with their job. My people may be ugly but are not without intelligence. You will be impressed, for you have a beautiful role in this plan."

"Your two hundred years of pain for humans?"

Zakamonsky nodded, regretfully. "Sometimes you need harsh medicine, but you will see it is the right medicine. Humans have ruined the Earth.

They need to be corrected, and they will be. Everything will work out right in the end - in two hundred years' time!"

Georgina snapped: "We have to stay in here for the next two hundred years while you show us how great your plans are? Two hundred years?"

Charlotte looked horrified, the magnitude of the situation becoming apparent.

Zakamonsky looked at them in a kindly manner.

"It may seem like two hundred years, may feel like two hundred years, but in reality, the show will last only a few hours. You will be immersed in every stage of the Earth as it evolves over the next two hundred years; a few hours only for this magnificent experience – three days at the most."

"Three days! This is outrageous! Let us go immediately!"

Zakamonsky shrugged. "Just relax. Immerse yourself in the experience… there is no other way."

Zakamonsky whisked himself to the exit. "I must leave now. I shall check in with you every now and then."

Then he was through the door, and there was a click as the door locked and the cinema sealed up.

Georgina immediately turned to Squires, "Squires, check the door!"

Squires advanced on the door. His fingers felt the lock; his fingers probed all around the door. "It is sealed ma'am, there is no way through this door."

"You are dematerialised – can you not walk through it and open it from the other side?"

"I wish I could, ma'am, but I cannot, because of my fingers. My fingers are material; they will block me. I have the worst of both worlds. Figgis, wait till I get my fingers on him. He will wish he had never been born…"

"Never mind about that, see if there is any other way out."

Squires quickly checked every crevice of the cinema and came to a blank. "No, ma'am, the cinema is completely sealed. We will have to wait until that Zakamonsky lets us out."

The cinema began to shake; the lights darkened.

An ominous echoing voice ricocheted around the room. "Are you sitting comfortably?" it boomed. "Now the show will begin!"

CHAPTER FIVE

1

Zakamonsky's show did not start at the beginning, but five years after his take-over of the planet. The girls were looking at the Earth in the aftermath of some momentous human catastrophe. Far and wide, humankind was stumbling around in a daze. Stunned populations everywhere, their appearance shabby, attire well worn. Suddenly they were in New York. Men in heavily soiled business suits were walking aimlessly down Fifth Avenue. There was no hustle and bustle, no rush hour; just a few confused, directionless humans in worn-out business suits, lumbering down Fifth Avenue. Hard to say where they were going, and who knew where the hordes of previous times had gone. Not many cars – a few abandoned in the middle of the road. The occasional car raced down the long, straight thoroughfare, avoiding the abandoned ones – impossible to see who was driving, maybe elites of some new order; shop windows not cleaned in years, the high-fashion Fifth Avenue shops deserted, mannequins blown over – their once-cutting-edge garments covered in dust; nobody in any shop. The massive New York skyscrapers towering up from the sidewalks were mainly intact: no destruction, simply covered in grey sheets of dust; windows not cleaned in years. Desolate, empty, unmaintained. Scaffolding hanging loose. The city almsot deserted; just a small number of people walking the streets in a daze.

It was the same in London, Paris, Moscow. Big Ben had stopped at three minutes past two; nobody had bothered to restart it. The vast Yangtze River in Shanghai; void of ships. The shopping mall in San Francisco: empty, all businesses boarded up. At cities towns and villages across the globe it was the same story: small, zombie-like populations walking the streets.

Charlotte, Georgina and Squires watched trying to retain some form of reality against the crushing influence of the red stone.

"What is going on?" Georgina shouted. "Mr Zakamonsky, what is going on? What has happened to these people?" She shouted this over and over. "Mr Zakamonsky, where are you, where are you?"

Finally Zakamonsky appeared a few feet away. "What is the matter, my dear?"

"What have you done to these people? What have you done to them? This is a horrible plan."

"It is the first stage in the rehabilitation of humans… nothing to worry about!"

"Has there been a war?"

"No war? No."

"A nuclear disaster?"

"No, nothing like that. Relax, don't worry! Everything is fine. Learn to relax."

"What has happened? I want to know – I need to know!"

2

"I have actually watched what happened," Fredrick said.

Hubert piped up: "Have you sir?"

"Yes, I sneaked into his palace and saw Zakamonsky's plans. This part was omitted from the presentation. It was very horrible."

"What happened?"

"The Zaki Family was made and released. Once per week it came on and populations around the world waited excitedly for the next episode. The hapless Zaki family were always trying to do the right thing and be accepted by humans, always messing up. People loved it; it was funny and emotional. Each week, Zakamonsky engaged thousands of market researchers to get information on how to make 'The Zaki Family' the ultimate comedy-heart-string-puller. It worked; almost the entire world became emotionally involved in the exploits of 'The Zaki Family'."

"What is so bad about that?"

"It is what happened next."

"What did happen next?"

"Zakamonsky had his special virus released."

"Oh."

"A thorough job was done so that almost the entire human population was infected. It was in the water; in the food; in body scans at airports: everywhere. Although nearly everyone was infected, not everyone had symptoms. The virus was designed with a switch that was controlled from outside. Zakamonsky controlled the switch, and he could choose who got symptoms and who did not."

"I suppose that is what Mr Zakamonsky meant by 'they will be putty in my hands'."

"I imagine that is what he did mean," Fredrick said grimly. "Zakamonsky had various features built into the virus, too. Features for his own entertainment: his favourite was the virus's control of the bowels. He planned to have a person evacuate their bowels at embarrassing moments for his own entertainment and laugh his head off."

"Disgusting! Let us hope Georgina Tipton manages to overpower him somehow."

"Let us hope so. The virus was unlike any virus the Earth had ever seen. Not a single scientist could explain it. For the overwhelming portion of the population, it was not fatal, just sneezing fits: constant sneezing for a few hours, then a break, then another sneezing fit. Very few were hospitalised. Zakamonsky waited a few weeks into this new pandemic before making his debut on the world stage."

"What did he do?"

"He came on the television. If you switched on almost any channel in the world, he was on it; giving his speech! It was easy because he had already replaced the heads of most television stations around the world."

"What did he say?"

"He was kindly and apologetic, and said: 'I am very sorry to tell you, but I have to reveal to you that The Zaki Family are a real family and they are living on Earth. I am extremely sorry to tell you that the virus is an alien virus and The Zaki Family brought it with them. They did not mean to. The good news is that because it is an alien virus, we know exactly how to deal with it: I have the cure.'"

"What happened?"

Populations were shocked as the realised 'The Zaki Family' were actually here on Earth. After the broadcast ended, there was worldwide outrage. Television stations were attacked; the Earth's population became furious. There were vows to track down Zakamonsky and 'The Zaki Family', and bring these snivelling aliens to task for bringing these sneezing fits to Earth.

Zakamonsky waited a day or two, then switched on a far more serious level of the virus. He gave this to millions of victims. Hospitals filled up. Field marquees were erected and Zakamonsky came back on television. He was more repentant than ever.

"I am really very sorry, but I do know how to deal with this. Please let my physicians into your hospitals and we can cure this terrible disease. Please let me show you my good faith to help you."

There was widespread suspicion, yet a few hospitals experimented with Zakamonsky's offer. Minutes after his physicians had treated the patients, the symptoms miraculously disappeared and the patients were as good as normal. More hospitals agreed to Zakamonsky's treatment: every patient made a full and rapid recovery. Very soon, every hospital was accepting Zakamonsky's treatment, and every patient recovered. Of course, the virus was still inside them; but switched off."

"What happened then?"

"After the initial shock, people sympathised with his mission and Zakamonsky became a hero. It is funny how quickly people come around to accepting a new situation. He explained his mission on television; he told the world the aliens were here to learn the beauty and graces of the Earth, to instigate these graces amongst their own people. They were here to improve themselves. By and large, people accepted this as a noble objective and let Zakamonsky get on with it. Then Zakamonsky made demands."

Hubert became bulldog-like: "Demands? What sort of demands?"

"Demands that large numbers of aliens be allowed to settle on Earth, and to run certain institutions. There was widespread shock. This time the human population said 'no', they would not accept this. There was universal protest that this should not be done. This time, Zakamonsky became ruthless. Turned on the virus back on full. Two-thirds of the population received sneezing fits. One-third of the population received the fatal level. Fatal. It was ghastly beyond belief."

"You mean…?"

Fredrick nodded. "It is very distressing how dictators can gain such a huge level of control simply by killing large numbers of people. It is the most despicable practice; something I would never do. To be fair, that was General Lout's part of the plan."

"This will not help the wooing process with Georgina."

"Maybe it is why he omitted it from the presentation."

"Does he still think he can woo Georgina?"

"I do not know. Let us watch and not talk. We see what happens."

3

"Tell me what has happened to these people!" Georgina shrieked at Zakamonsky.

"You do not need to know my dear; it is all for the greater good."

"I do need to know."

"What you need to do is relax; you will be well looked after."

"Why do you not tell me?"

"You are not involved in this part of the operation; I care about your welfare so much. Let me show you how much I care about you."

"No!"

"Calm down. Let me show you!"

With that, the experimental theatre came did its magic, and like some super-simulator they were transported. Transported into a glittering palace in the Himalayas!

4

The palace was the height of opulence: sparkling crystals everywhere; walls encrusted with jewels; lavish rooms fifty feet high; intricate mosaics; fountains cascading down into silver pools. Servants led Georgina's party through a series of splendid rooms into a pampering parlour. This, too, was the height of luxury: extreme softness and padding. They were ushered into sumptuously cushioned reclining chairs while the servants washed their feet and a masseur came with warmed oils ready to rub in.

Squires followed them. "Getting your feet done, are you? Here I am with no body while you get your feet done," he said.

Georgina sympathised. "None of this was my idea, Mr Squires. I shall do what I can to return you to a full-body situation."

"Thank you, ma'am, yes, thank you."

Warm air was rising through air ducts in the floor while two servants gently waved giant fans, giving a smooth, cooling air flow. Two more servants appeared and handed extensive menus to Charlotte and Georgia, and the first servant reverently asked of Charlotte: "If Madam could browse the menu and let me know what she requires for her midday meal, and what time her food is desired? Please order now so I can inform the cookery staff to prepare the fare to perfection at the appropriate time." He said, graciously bowing.

Charlotte whispered to Georgina: "Wow, this is amazing."

Georgina dismissed her own waiter and said, "He is trying to fool us, trying to buy us."

"Stop being grumpy! This is fabulous. Mr Zakamonsky is treating us beyond our wildest dreams. Look at the menu: we've hit the jackpot!"

"What about those people walking on Fifth Avenue? They were like zombies?"

"What people?"

"You really don't remember?"

"No. What people?"

One of the properties of the red stone was to blur memories to the point of forgetting what had come before. It intensified the moment to a point where the past was almost a blank; it was one of the reasons Zakamonsky was able to control his people so effectively. Charlotte had forgotten, but Georgina was making a valiant effort to keep remembering: being a warrior of resistance.

She impressed upon Charlotte: "The people on Fifth Avenue. They were walking like zombies; he has done something with them. We must find out and stop it."

Charlotte looked blankly. "You always said the moment is what matters – that we should live in the 'now'."

"Not if it blinds us to what came before."

"Let's just enjoy the now for once." Charlotte looked around the heavenly room, the servants, the oils, the menu. "I intend to enjoy every moment; it is fabulous. I have never known anything like it! The pleasure of absolute luxury. Loosen up, it is fantastic."

Charlotte went on to order dinner.

Georgina threw her arms up in despair, "You are no help at all! Mr Zakamonsky. "

"Zakamonsky! Zakamonsky!" she screamed. She screamed again and again.

After few minutes of screaming, he appeared.

"What is it, my dear?"

"You are trying to buy us…prevent us from seeing what is happening."

"Not buy you – protect you from this difficult transition period. Trying to give you the best in this unhappy time for the Earth."

"I do not want to be pampered while the Earth suffers. I want to do my duty."

"I admire a sense of duty. That is one of the things I most admire about you."

"Why are you doing this? Giving us all this luxury? Why are you bothering with me? There must be millions of women at your service, doing their duty."

Because…." He stuttered. "Because…" He stuttered a little more. "Because, I love you," he said.

"You love me?"

He simply said 'yes', and Georgina was stunned. It was some little while before she said, "Is that so?"

Zakamonsky bowed his head slowly. "Yes it is. You are the first person I ever loved."

Georgina looked at him closely, and found a deep ancestral longing in his eyes, and was amazed to see an almost child-like need, and that what he was saying was genuine. Looking into his eyes, she felt herself going dizzy with a feeling of compassion.

Zakamonsky nodded meekly. "I am sorry, but it is true. I have never known love in my life: my first experience. To be truthful, I feel a little naked. It is a risky situation to admit this. I do not know if I can trust you."

Georgina rapidly assessed the situation, trying to keep hold of herself. She looked at his face, and it was like a little boy pleading for help.

"Can I trust you? I want to know," he repeated.

Georgina was stunned. Deep in his eyes, she could see he had been absolutely starved of love. His harshness and cruelty was down to the complete emptiness of ever having received love, and he was pleading for it: pleading for love; pleading to be whole, and he was asking this of her. This was so sudden, so unexpected. Was this her mission in life? To tame Zakamonsky?

Georgina tried to calculate whether going on a perilous journey with Zakamonsky could change him; perhaps change the course of human history. Perhaps humans would not go through whatever Zakamonsky was planning for them. But could it put her in danger?

"If I go on a journey with you, will you respect me?"

"Respect you?"

"Respect my body and respect me as a person? I will only go on a journey with you if you agree to these things."

Zakamonsky looked into her eyes. “You are the most beautiful thing I have ever seen. I will agree to those things.”

“I insist that you listen to me and respect my opinions, too.”

“Is that how it works?”

“Yes, that is how it works.”

“I want to experience love. I have experienced a little with you. I will do what it takes to experience more,” Zakamonsky said, with his pleading little eyes.

Georgina was thoughtful for a while and cautiously responded.

“If you want me to guide you through the most wonderful mysterious adventure of love, the most precious commodity of human existence, you must respect me and treat me as an equal partner. Once we let go, we will both be at the mercy of love.”

“I see.” Zakamonsky was thoughtful. “You must understand I am on the most important mission of my entire being. In my long existence I have never experienced love, so this is difficult. I am master of my species, anointed to this role. I am bigger and more superior than any of my species, and my life span is five thousand years to their one thousand years. I can reveal I am in my fifth millcnnium, nearing the end of my reign. You may be surprised to learn I am four thousand, five hundred years of age. This could be my last mission, the zenith of my career. I am becoming an old man, Georgina. Now I have met you I have never felt this way. I could be a happy man and experience another avenue of life that I never knew existed: love. It is more than that; it must be destiny – there is no other way to explain it. You must see my mission and join me on it. Together, we can create a glorious future for the Earth."

"What will be the glorious future of the Earth?"

"Come on the journey and you will see."

"What will my role be in this glorious future?"

"The ultimate role: the empress of the entire Earth. After the transition period ends, you will have this role."

"And during the transition period?"

"I can offer you a magnificent role; a role where you can exercise your duty to humanity, your commitment to enlightening the human race."

"What is that about?"

"My dear, you are upsetting my presentation. You are not permitting me to show all the delights this palace has to offer. Never mind: I will show you your role. It is a vital role in this transition period of the Earth. Simply sit back and I will transport you into your glorious role."

Georgina, with a leap of faith, relaxed into the plush, reclining seat of the pampering parlour and was transported; Charlotte and Squires as well. Transported onto a barge: the Imperial Earth Barge, the largest, most beautiful barge in the history of Earth. Zakamonsky's intentions for her were truly surprising.

5

The Imperial Earth Barge was over one thousand feet long, with a huge upturned nose like a giant gondolier. It gracefully whisked through the water, propelled by ten thousand rowers, and was gliding down the Ganges River. The sides of the boat were adorned by hundreds of thousands of candles flickering in translucent containers and illuminating its regal passage. On top sat Georgina with her entourage, but she was illuminated the brightest of all.

In the Ganges waters, and on its banks, millions from the sub-continent awaited the arrival of the barge. Some had walked a thousand miles for this. Some had waited in the river for weeks. As the boat approached, they were overcome with ecstasy. They bowed and prayed to Georgina. Zakamonsky was beside Georgina in the shadows.

"Why are they praying to me?" she asked.

"Because they love you. You are the light of their lives. They want you to inspire them; it is your duty to inspire them. Do this and give them hope to carry on. They are worshipping you as the Goddess Ganga."

"I am not the Goddess Ganga."

"Maybe you are. Maybe you can find the Goddess Ganga within you. Shine out with the Goddess Ganga, give them light and hope – fulfil their expectations. Help them through this difficult transition period."

"How do I become Goddess Ganga if I am not her?"

"In you are the attributes necessary to become the Goddess Ganga. We are Gods and we can access these attributes. Purity and purification are some of the attributes of the Goddess Ganga. Find the purity and purification powers within you and become the Goddess Ganga."

"Purity and purification?"

"Yes – isn't that a noble cause? Purity and purification. Is that not what mankind needs? Purification from the madness of the past few centuries; purification in order to realise the true essence of life on Earth. Humans need to be reset to experience this, the true essence of life on Earth."

Georgina was surprised. "Is that your vision for humans? To find the true essence of life on Earth?"

Zakamonsky simply said, "Yes … try to find the purity within you … the powers to inspire purification. They are within you. Then you can become the Goddess Ganga. Be the Goddess Ganga. That is what they are looking for."

Georgina took Zakamonsky's words to heart and tried to access this reservoir of purity; a fountain of uncontaminated purpose; a well of freshness.

"I think I am finding it."

Zakamonsky was pleased and said, "wonderful" and adorned her with a beautiful white gown embroidered in yellows. He wrapped her in garlands, and the crowds below took off and roared. Not a little roar: a gigantic thunder of ecstasy, and its roar travelled many miles down the Ganges River.

"Concentrate on that fountain of purity within you; let it flow and get bigger."

The more she listened to Zakamonsky, the more she found this well within her and it came flooding out.

"Stand up and bless them!" Zakamonsky said.

She rose and raised her arms and another explosion of ecstasy rang from the crowds. She felt a union of bliss and purity between her and the multitudes below. Zakamonsky was most pleased.

"I knew it," he said. "You truly are the one; I knew you could be the one. You have confirmed it. You too have all the power of the Gods within you. We shall rule the Earth together; it is destiny. The Earth has waited millions of years for this. We shall bring the Earth to its true destiny. We shall unveil a new age for the Earth. Together, we shall do this. An age of true happiness."

Georgina was overcome with this revelation, suddenly realising this was her destiny: to bring the Golden Age of Earth into being with Zakamonsky.

Zakamonsky nodded. "It is a surprise to me, too. Together, fulfilling the destiny of our lives! Maybe you could make me a happy man for my final years. Love: could you be in love with me? Is that possible? Could you teach me love?"

It was the surprise of Georgina's life. She looked into his little-boy eyes. "Yes, Mr Zakamonsky, I think I can."

"Thank you! Thank you, Gina – thank you from the depths of my soul."

She looked through his little-boy eyes and realised he was starved of love, and felt she could love him. Love started flowing out of her, and she lurched over to kiss him, but he backed away.

"Not here, never in public. We are rulers with great duties to fulfil. Our love must be in private. I long to fulfil our love, am anxious to learn and share this love, but not during our duties."

Georgina felt an enormous respect. His stalwart dedication to duty: love in private, duty in public. These were her exact values too. She knew then that she had met her true match.

The barge sailed on and Georgina performed her duty dispensing purity and tools for purification to the multitudes below. In return, she felt their thanks and adoration.

"This is more than I expected. I am ready to do my duties," she said.

Zakamonsky nodded proudly. "I have access to all the secrets and strategies of the Gods and I will teach them to you," he said.

The barge sailed on and she blessed the crowds. In moments when the barge sailed through rocky straights and the multitudes were not in attendance, they touched each other: a touch tender and electric. A great, tumultuous love was slowly erupting. These interludes were 'oh so short' and the adoring crowds were once more on the banks, demanding of Georgina of what they needed.

"When our duties are not so great we shall be together more and more," Zakamonsky whispered.

"Yes, I want that," Georgina said.

Along the Ganges; they found more opportunities to let their love grow. After a few weeks, they came to the end of the Ganges and sailed into the Bay of Bengal.

"We shall sail the Earth and I shall teach you to be Goddess to all peoples on this planet," Zakamonsky said.

Zakamonsky was true to his word. They sailed through Myanmar and through the rivers of Asia. Georgina learnt that every country and every region was endowed with its own spirit; an aspect of God that resonated with its peoples. It was embedded in the land. Most people had forgotten and become disconnected from the spirit of their land, but Zakamonsky knew, and taught it to Georgina. And Georgina accessed it within her and gave it to the people. And the people exalted.

"You see, my dear, every one of these Gods and Goddesses is inside you. That is the secrets of the Gods. Many different Gods but really only one: one God with many flavours. A flavour for every country on Earth, and every one of these flavours is inside you! That is the secret of the Gods. That is why we are ideally suited to rule the Earth and usher in the incredible tapestry of harmony of Earth."

Georgina was amazed at her good fortune. She always knew she was special, but it had taken Zakamonsky to unlock the powers within her. And she was in love; it was the most-good-fortune anyone could wish for.

The sailed across Europe, and sailed through the Americas. Georgina was in a blissful state. Not only was she giving her subjects enlightenment and receiving their love in return, but also enjoying a personal love with Zakamonsky: the hidden aspect of Zakamonsky. The outcome could not have been sweeter. Oh, the joy of discovering one's true destiny and the ecstasy of finding an unexpected love that promised undiscovered depths.

They sailed through every country in Africa and on to Australia. Then south-east Asia. Nearly every country on Earth was visited.

When this was completed Zakamonsky said to her, "My love, I must leave. I have duties and responsibilities of my own to discharge. I have taught you secrets of the Gods. Now you must discharge your divine role. Continue to visit each country and give the peoples what they need. We must both discharge our duties. I shall see you soon, my love."

6

Zakamonsky left and Georgina sailed on. She sailed around the world and everywhere the majestic barge went, adoring crowds were there to greet her.

She sailed around the world again. Then again. Again and again.

The years went by, the Earth evolved; she longed to see Zakamonsky, but he was always busy. She began to feel like some grand mariner, destined to roam the seas for ever. She called out to Zakamonsky but no answer came, and began to think he had abandoned her. She became distraught, but on and on she sailed, doing her duty. Finally he answered.

"My dear, I have been busy. Soon we shall be together, together forever. Be patient; you must really be patient, for the outcome is superb, and we will be together."

This brightened her and gave her hope.

She sailed on. Everywhere the barge went it sailed through adoring crowds: pleading crowds, crowds praying to be released from their suffering. The years went by. Zakamonsky had given her five hundred years of human life. It was now seventy-five years since the journey had begun, and she was becoming weary. The barge sailed up the Humber River in northern England.

Many times she had sailed up the Humber River. It was twenty years since her last visit. Much had changed – so much. The City of Hull was no longer. Ploughed over and cultivated as open fields. The odd ruin peeped up from the fields; tips of landmarks like haunting reminders of the city that had once existed. Haunting, haunting. Men and women were working the fields, and had been reduced to savage living. Barely clothed, hairy. As the barge approached, the multitudes looked up and cried out "Boudica, Boudica save us!"

The barge sailed up the river, avoiding the twisted remains of the once-immense Humber Bridge. On the banks, working the fields, were chain gangs, gangs of dishevelled, half-naked humans chained together in gangs of over one hundred. Some gangs were working the fields; other gangs were being marched to other destinations; some to quarries. They were beaten by their guards as they marched, beaten by Zakamonsky's warrior aliens. Hard aliens: vicious thugs. They whipped their charges mercilessly and were taking pleasure in it.

Georgina was shocked beyond belief. She screamed out to Zakamonsky. "Zakamonsky you have tricked me! Come here! Come here immediately!"

Zakamonsky did not respond. She called him again and again. She felt herself sinking, but also a rising fury: a determination to reverse whatever had happened. She called again. And again. Finally he responded, appearing a few feet from her on the helm of the barge. "Yes?" he said.

"Why are your aliens treating my people in such an appalling way?"

"They are keeping order. It is essential to keep order in these uncertain times. There has been a rebellion."

"Rebellion or no rebellion, I do not want my people treated this way. We need to resolve this in a reasonable way."

There was a hardness about Zakamonsky: a steely hardness she had not witnessed before.

"Our duty is not to argue with base agitators, but to govern. To govern, do you understand? General Lout has suggested this strategy. He is a good organiser. I must govern for the greater good of all. This is what you must learn and understand."

"No, this is wrong! I forbid it!"

"You are in no position to forbid. I have my duties – you have yours. I must discharge my duties and you, yours. Let me get on with mine."

"No! Please, let us talk about this."

"At the end of the transition period we shall talk. It lasts for two hundred years. You have done seventy-five years. There are one hundred and twenty-five years to go. Then we shall talk. I have extended five hundred years of your life: be patient!"

"That will be too late. I want the suffering of humans to stop now."

"No," Zakamonsky said, and left.

Zakamonsky was gone and the barge sailed on, sailed on automatically, and Georgina realised she was powerless. She could not stop the barge or stop the suffering. "Boudicca, Boudicca," some of the people shouted. She had no power; she was no Boudicca – simply a figurehead to pacify them. Zakamonsky had completely outfoxed her.

The boat sailed on, through England, through Scotland and Ireland; through the Americas north and south; through Africa; through Asia. There were chain gangs throughout the entire world. Everywhere, there had been rebellions and everywhere they were harshly supressed, Zakamonsky's thugs beating the rebellion out of all of them.

Charlotte and Squires were still with Georgina on the helm of the barge, and they watched on in stunned silence; although Squires did offer to strangle Zakamonsky upon his return.

Zakamonsky's grip on the Earth was total. The majority of humans had succumbed, obediently following General Lout's orders; they had no option. The ones that rebelled were put in chain gangs, or in camps, or were tortured.

Much of the human population now worked in the fields, cultivating crops. The fields all had watchtowers with aliens stationed up high, with machine guns trained to shoot humans who disrupted production. It was the same in factories. It was far worse for rebels. Georgina witnessed rebels being experimented upon: humans wired up to monitor pain thresholds as legs were routinely sewn off; heads opened up, probing limits of pain on the brain. This catastrophe for humans was so extreme, the degradation so complete, that Georgina could stand it no longer. "Mama!" she called out, "Mama, where are you?" A little while later, Nefeli appeared on the helm, a frail little figure, her thin, white dress torn and billowing. She said: "What is it my child? What is the matter?"

"Look what has happened. Zakamonsky has taken over the Earth. He said he loved me, but has tricked me. He is cruel, he is a maniac! See what he has done!"

Nefeli watched the chain gangs as the barge sailed along: the fields, the watchtowers. She watched this with a growing defiance. "You need to stop him, my child. Do you have the stone?"

"Yes," Georgina extracted it from her velvet purse.

It shone a deep, powerful blood red and Nefeli recoiled. "Zakamonsky has you in his power through the influence of the red stone. You must neutralise this stone and be released from Zakamonsky's power."

"How can I neutralise the stone?"

"Through the power of the white stone, remember?"

"Oh, the white stone. Yes, I remember. It is inside the trunk in Arizona. How are we going to get hold of it?"

Nefeli rose up. "I will visit your grandfather. He must get it for you. He has been an arrogant man for most of his life. This time I will see him, and he must listen! He will get it. George William, I am coming for you!" She shouted this as loud and with as much defiance as her frail voice would allow.

CHAPTER SIX

1

George William was sitting with Figgis on the sun terrace of their Greek Island villa, and instructing Figgis with things to do for the business of the day. While doing this, he was sipping at a rare scotch whiskey.

"There is an interesting story about this whiskey," Fredrick said.

"Should we not concentrate on helping with the rescue mission?" Hubert replied, with some desperation.

"I told you before, we are here to observe," Fredrick snapped. "Observe and see which party prevails. Now let me get on with the story about the Scotch whiskey."

"Very well, sir," Hubert said, with an impatient reluctance.

"You will remember there is a monastery up the hill that is full of weird characters: monks of some description."

"Yes, I remember some mention of a monastery."

"Well, these monks like dressing up as Greek Gods. Whether they think themselves as heirs to the various Greek Gods or just like dressing up, I am not sure. One of them, who calls himself Heracles, liked sitting in the garden beyond

Georgina Tipton's terrace. He was besotted by Georgina and her party. He was respectful of George William because of his royal heritage, but never sat in his garden; only sat in Georgina's garden. It was the mystique of Georgina he was interested in. Sometimes he would pass by George William's garden in order to reach an olive grove, and bring back a basket full of olives to the monastery. On one occasion, as he was passing the garden, George William called out to him, 'Hey Hercules, come over here.'…."

Heracles nervously approached George William and gave a little bow. "It is Heracles, your Majesty," he corrected. "Heracles!"

"Yes, of course. Hercules was the Roman; Heracles is the original."

Heracles bowed and gave a little smile.

"Anyway, Heracles, I want some whiskey."

Heracles was puzzled. "Whiskey?"

"Yes, a rare Scotch whiskey. I think the nearest place it could be found would be Athens. I want a bottle."

"You want a bottle of rare Scotch whiskey which can be found in Athens?"

"You have summed it up precisely. Would you get me a bottle?"

Heracles thought for a moment. "I shall have to consult with the brothers," he said.

Heracles consulted and came back later on. "The brothers have agreed. A party of four of us will take our fishing boat and get the bottle of whiskey. We shall set out tonight and return the day after tomorrow."

"No, I don't want you to go by boat. I want you to swim."

"Swim?" Heracles was horrified.

George William retorted. "Are you Heracles or not? That is the question."

Heracles returned to the brotherhood and came back to George a few hours later.

"The brotherhood have agreed. They shall accompany me on the fishing boat. I shall swim five kilometres and they shall resuscitate me each time, then I will do another five kilometres. The journey shall take ten days."

"That is good, Heracles. Well done. Off you go! Have a pleasant journey!"

Heracles went on his arduous journey and Figgis said, "Is this not a bit cruel sir? Sending the geezer on a round trip, swimming two hundred miles?"

"Nonsense. He would have a rest in Athens; it would be good for him, and clarify whether he wanted to be Heracles or not. I would get a decent bottle of whiskey, too!"

Ten days later, the party returned. They were windswept, weather beaten, and Heracles was on the verge of collapse through exhaustion.

"I have the bottle of whiskey," Heracles said, handing it over.

George looked at the bottle. "Very good. This looks an excellent whiskey. Are you feeling more like Heracles now?"

Heracles shrugged, not saying anything.

"Next time I want you to swim ten kilometres before taking a rest, and bring me two bottles of whiskey."

"Next time?"

"The whiskey is not going to bring itself; you have to do it. Heracles would not flinch. Do you want to be Heracles?"

He nodded, nervously.

"I think you can do it. I believe you have the fortitude and strength to do it. With sufficient training, it is possible you could perform great and wonderful feats."

Although weary, Heracles brightened, and left with his party to contemplate.

"That is basically the story," Fredrick said, "and that is how George William gets his whiskey."

"Thank you for telling me that, sir. Very interesting."

"Now we should see where George William is up to with his business, and see whether he will go and rescue Georgina.

2

"What are the numbers, Figgis?"

"What numbers are you on about?"

"World leaders: how many have you replaced? How many are we up to?"

"It is a lot of work replacing world leaders."

"Yes, yes!"

"I hope you appreciate what I am doing, and how much work it is."

"Yes, yes! What are the numbers?"

"Twenty-four; two down from yesterday."

"Two down? How is that possible?"

"Well, I replaced three world leaders today. It was a lot of work I can tell you, but overnight Mr Zakamonsky replaced five of my world leaders with five of his world leaders."

"Well, that is bloody marvellous isn't it? As soon as we replace a world leader, Zakamonsky comes along and replaces it with one of his. At this rate, let us see, it will take fourteen days and we will have zero leaders, and Zakamonsky will have the lot."

"Not quite like that, sir. Mr Zakamonsky had a bit of luck last night; besides, I am going to put in more security. I have been discussing this with Chief Robot Robert."

"Since you and Zakamonsky both use Robert to make the robots, is it not logical the Chief Robot Robert will simply tell Zakamonsky what security is in place?"

"No chance of that!" Figgis said indignantly, "Chief Robot Robert respects me wholeheartedly." Figgis took a moment or two to think this through. "It is probably true that Mr Zakamonsky will ask Chief Robot Robert to find a way to override the security and Chief Robot Robert will be obligated to supply this. However, if that happens, I will always be a day ahead. I estimate my daily tally of world leaders will always be one up on Mr Zakamonsky's."

George William shook his head and downed some more whiskey. "It seems a losing battle, but I suppose it does not really matter because we need to do away with the system of having so many leaders; gets too complicated. We need just one leader: me. I have the plan the world needs. This is a very fine whiskey, Figgis, you should try some."

"No thank you, sir."

"Most of the leaders are a bunch of deadheads. It would not surprise me if half these world leaders were robots."

Figgis stared at him like a thunder bolt had hit him.

"Sir, I think you are right!"

"What do you mean, Figgis?"

"I think many of the world leaders could already be robots. I had a message from Chief Robot Robert. It was about the British Prime Minister; the one we abducted two days ago. They had a problem locating his brain. Like he did not have one; like he was a robot."

"The British Prime Minister did not have a brain?"

"No."

"You mean some of the world leaders could already have been robots before we and Zakamonsky started replacing them with our robots?"

"Yes, sir, that's right."

George William grimaced, trying to get his head around these silly technologies that human populations had so willingly embraced. "Figgis, let us find out if the British Prime Minister is in fact a robot. This is something we need to know."

"Yes, sir. I shall contact Chief Robot Robert right away."

Figgis got Chief Robot Robert up on his screen who greeted him with reverence.

"It is an honour to be in your presence," the giant robot said. The whole of his massive structure from waist upwards, hands, chest and arms began bowing, bowing repeatedly; his upper frame going up and down in bowing mode. "You are the esteemed Aloysius Figgis: my founder, my creator. You are the wise one, the revered one. You are Mr Aloysius Figgis, the honourable!"

Figgis glowed with pride. George William flipped his eyes. "Why is he doing that, Figgis?"

"He appreciates me," Figgis growled. "Someone around here appreciates me, and I like that. I like being appreciated." He said this last bit poignantly.

Robert finished the routine, and Figgis said to him, "Robert we need to confirm if the British Prime Minister was already a robot."

"Yes, Your Greatness," Chief Robot Robert replied. "That operation was carried out by a commando force from our base in Mildenhall England; it was headed by a commander I called Jimmy."

"He's called Jimmy?"

"Named after your cat that sadly died."

"Thank you Robert, that is thoughtful."

Commander Jimmy came on the screen. Robert asked him, "Commander Jimmy – was the British Prime Minister already a robot?"

"Yes," Commander Jimmy said. "Yes, he was. We examined him, and the British Prime Minster was already a fully functioning robot. We disconnected the operating system, but retained his motor functions. It has unique features – let me demonstrate his eating function. "

Jimmy carried the inanimate, rather overweight, prime minster and stood him up, activating his eating function. Jimmy produced a carrot and fed it into the prime minister's mouth. The Prime Minister chewed the carrot. "You will observe the prime minister chews food exactly as the human prime minister would; it is very well observed."

"That is clever, Jimmy. Very clever. Isn't that clever, sir?"

"Eating a carrot? Yes, I suppose it is."

The prime minister finished chewing and digested the carrot.

Figgis asked, "Where does the food go after he has chewed it?"

"I am glad you asked that: it travels down the torso to a waste disposal unit." Jimmy indicated the direction of travel with a pointing stick.

"Oh, that is clever! Is that clever, sir?"

"Yes, I suppose it is."

"What happens when the waste disposal gets full?"

"You are talking about the emptying?" Jimmy asked.

Figgis nodded. "Yes."

Jimmy turned the prime minister around. "I am glad you asked." He pulled the prime minister's trousers down, exposing his bare buttocks. "You will observe there is a little catch on each cheek of the buttock, enabling them to open. When each cheek is fully open, the tray can be released and emptied." He undid both catches and, like double doors, each cheek sprung open. He pulled out a tray. "It is as simple as that."

"Oh, that is clever. Very clever – isn't that clever, sir?"

"Yes, yes – I have got the point. Close the prime minister up now!"

"Jimmy…what if we had a push-to-release system instead of catches?"

"It might be difficult if he sits down. We risk having his bottom flying open when he is sitting down or dining; it might not look right if the prime minister's bottom opens up during a state banquet."

"What if he is just walking?"

"Again, the action rubbing against his trousers could activate the whole apparatus. It is a spring-loaded mechanism; his bottom could burst straight though his trousers as he is walking."

"That is interesting. Maybe we could modify the design?"

"All right, Figgis – that is enough. Enough of the prime minister's buttocks; do your design talk some other time. Thank you, Jimmy. Thank you, Robert – we have established what we need to know. Figgis, shut down your device!"

Figgis closed off the screen, still intrigued by the system. "For the moment we need to keep the prime minister decent. If we introduce more compression, we could reduce the emptying time…"

George William snapped: "Stop! Never mind about waste disposal or anything to do with the prime minister's bottom - we have some very serious issues here! There is someone else in the frame who is replacing world leaders. If it is not you, and not Zakamonsky – who is it?"

"I don't know."

George William took another glug of whiskey and paced about the terrace, thinking about this.

"If there is already someone out there, trying to manipulate world events, the question is: what is he trying to do?"

"It could be a she."

"You are right: it could be a she. There is some shadowy figure doing very strange things. This would explain the world-wide response to this pandemic. The only conclusion that can be drawn is that he, or she, is attempting to take over the world. The question is, who are they and what are they trying to do?"

"I don't know."

"Well think, dammit, Figgis!"

"Right-oh, sir."

"Have a big, deep think. Can you do a deep think?"

"Yes."

"Well, have one now."

"Right-oh."

Figgis started thinking: a big, deep one. Then Nefeli appeared on the scene.

She popped up at the end of the terrace, her thin white dress torn.

George was very surprised and exclaimed, "Nefeli!"

"George William, I am coming for you!" Nefeli said, purposefully advancing towards him.

"Steady on ole' girl! We are in the middle of some very important business. We are trying to find out who is replacing all the world leaders."

"You are a stupid, stupid man," she said. Now close to him, she began bashing him with a rolled-up newspaper.

George William was stunned. "What is going on? What have I done?"

"Do you know where our great-granddaughters are?"

"I imagine they are on their terrace on the other side of the house, about to start their afternoon aperitifs." He rose his glass. "Would you like to join me in a whiskey and calm yourself down? Figgis, get Nefeli a glass!"

"You are a stupid, stupid ignorant man."

"Steady on!"

"They are not on the other side of the house. They are with Zakamonsky in Los Angeles; he is holding them under the influence of the red stone."

"With Zakamonsky? Really? That is terrible!"

"Yes, with Zakamonsky, you ignorant man. You need to get the white stone and release them."

George William was mystified. "The white stone?"

"The white stone is the antidote. It will neutralise the effects of the red stone."

Figgis's ears pricked up. "There is a white stone?" he asked.

Nefeli said, "Yes! The white stone will neutralise the red stone. It will neutralise any realm the stone enters into."

"We need to get hold of the white stone, sir."

"I am sorry, Nefeli; you are right," George William said, becoming surprisingly humble. "I have been a fool. Where do we find the white stone?"

"It is in the trunk that Charles Tipton brought to America."

Figgis sad, "The trunk is still in Arizona,"

"Yes, Figgis, I know that." George William turned back to Nefeli. "I am sorry, Nefeli – sorry for everything that has happened. How did your dress get torn?"

Nefeli glared at him, silently, poignantly. "Just get the white stone and deliver it to the girls. Do you understand?" She started to fade away. "Just do it," she said, and disappeared.

George William turned to Figgis. "I suppose we had better get the white stone," he said.

"Yes, sir. I shall get the helicopter ready."

CHAPTER SEVEN

1

Figgis flew the helicopter to Athens International Airport where they boarded their private Learjet. Figgis raced the little jet down the Aegean into the Mediterranean. George William sat in the passenger cabin, taking stock of the situation – brooding – Zakamonsky seemed to be getting another one up on him.

Figgis raced through the Mediterranean and stopped mid-Atlantic for fuel. While refueling, Figgis got a message on his control panel. It read: 'Stop replacing my robots with your robots or I will turn the Earth dark purple!'

"They want turn the world purple."

George William scratched his head. "Who wants to turn the world purple?"

"The other party; the other party with the robots. They are threatening to turn the Earth dark purple."

"Zakamonsky wants to turn the Earth dark purple. Why?"

"Not Mr Zakamonsky, no! The other party: the third party. They will turn the Earth dark purple unless I stop replacing their robots."

"Well, that is bloody marvellous isn't it? I have a psychopath who has kidnapped my granddaughters, and now some imbecile who wants to turn the world purple." George William was wondering why he bothered pitching to come back to Earth.

Figgis asked, "What shall we do about it?"

"Nothing!" George said irritably. "We will keep everything as it is. We have an important mission in front of us to rescue the girls; that is what we shall do. Nothing else!"

The plane finished refuelling and took off. They continued in silence for an hour or two. George William contemplated the mad complexity of trying to run the Earth, and was beginning to think it was a losing battle. "Our job right now is to rescue the girls," he insisted.

They reached the initial, thin island of the Bahamas and Figgis pointed the little jet into the Gulf of Mexico. They hit the Mexican mainland and continued, flying low and fast, until they reached the border of southern Arizona. They were now just a few minutes away from the fortress. George William thought of a new problem.

"How are we going to get in there?"

"What do you mean, sir?"

"How are we going to get into the fortress? Zakamonsky has got the place under siege with his robots: our robots that he captured. They are in the desert surrounding the fortress – two million of them!"

"Good point. I shall have a think."

"Yes, you have a good think."

Figgis came up with an idea: "What about getting dematerialised? Then we will be invisible and the robots will not be able to see us. I have the dematerialising gun with me."

"Invisible like Squires?"

"Yes, a bit like Squires."

"I am not very keen on that idea, Figgis."

"It is perfectly safe, I know what I am doing."

"Squires does not think so. He is very upset. Wants his body back. Don't blame him; he is stuck with having just a pair of fingers."

"It will not be like that. I have not rematerialised Squires because I don't want him to beat me up."

"I have the solution," George William said, "you go first! You try it out and see how it goes."

All of a sudden, Figgis was not as keen as he had been. "I am flying the plane – I need my hands to fly the plane."

"I have a solution for that, too. You can dematerialise everything except your hands…it will be just like Squires."

"Hmmm," Figgis was a bit cornered with this. "Very well, I shall dematerialise myself."

"Good!"

George William watched, intrigued, as Figgis took density measurements all over his body, then proceeded to dematerialise himself with the gun. He did his feet and legs first. "You will join me after I am dematerialised? You will join me by being dematerialised, too?"

"Yes, yes! Get on with it Figgis."

Figgis dematerialised his privates and all up his body, and George William watched, fascinated, as Figgis's body slowly disappeared. His head vanished. Everything gone, except his hands.

"It is done, sir. Now it is your turn."

George William was a little confused. "How is it possible you can speak if you have no head?"

"Advanced physics sir. It will take ten and a half hours to explain. Do you want me to start now?"

"No Figgis, not now."

"Right sir, it is now your go." Figgis raised the gun in George William's direction.

George William got up. "I have many notes to write up first. I have business to do!" He quickly took off to the passenger cabin. Figgis followed with his hands holding the dematerialisation gun in aiming position. He pinned him down by one of the passenger seats.

"Come on, sir. Let's play fair. You do not want me to dematerialise you while you are moving about, it could go horribly wrong – horribly wrong!"

"Very well, Figgis, you win. Are you sure this dematerialisation thing is safe?"

"Look at me. I am OK."

There was not much to look at, just a pair of hands, and George William resigned himself to being dematerialised. "Come on Figgis, let us get it done."

George remained very still – perhaps he was praying – while Figgis dematerialised him. It did not take very long; maybe a minute or two. When it was done, George was surprised to discover that it was fine. He could hear, see, even smell. All his body was dematerialised except his hands.

"Aren't you doing my hands?"

"No, sir. We need the hands to handle the white stone physically; we cannot risk anything going wrong, not like it did with the Earth stone. We should not dematerialise the white stone, but handle it physically, without dematerialising it."

"That makes sense, Figgis, yes. Why do you think the Earth stone rematerialised the way it did?"

"If I knew, I would put it right. It is not made from Earth materials – that is why Earth physics do not work. It is composed of very special materials, the secret bedrock of the universe. The white stone must be made of the same materials; materials I do not understand. We cannot afford to have it go the same way as the Earth stone."

"You are right. We should not dematerialise the white stone; it could be a disaster. You are sure you will be able to rematerialise me successfully when this is over?"

"I hope so, sir."

"What do you mean, you 'hope so'?"

"Well, I have not actually done it with a human yet – Squires would have been the first one."

"Well, that is bloody marvellous isn't it? Now you tell me!"

"Did not want to worry you."

"This is very irresponsible, Figgis," George William said with a trace of panic. "Very irresponsible indeed! We could rematerialise as some kind of freak. Or a pigeon!"

"Wouldn't that be fun sir?"

"No it would not."

"Don't worry about it. Let us enjoy the way we are: invisible, just hands." Figgis glided his hands through the air. "We could snoop around like secret agents. Wouldn't that be fun? Secret agents."

"No, it would not and I do not want to be a secret agent. We simply need to retrieve the white stone and get out of here."

"Don't be so grumpy."

George William groaned. He was stuck with this moron with the mentality of a ten-year-old and could do absolutely nothing about it. He pointed out something else: "Although Zakamonsky's robots would not be able to see us, surely they would see the plane?"

"Yes, they would see the plane. What about it?"

"Well, if they see the plane, surely they must think someone is flying it."

"Yes."

"Would that not signify that someone has come to the fortress? Namely: us!"

"No, it would not do that. The robots are only alerted to look for three things: humans, other robots and bananas."

"Bananas?"

"Bananas are a decoy."

"Have you got any bananas on board?"

"I do not think so."

"Shall we search the aircraft? Let us do a thorough search and see if there are any bananas anywhere?"

"There are not any bananas on board."

"Are you sure?"

"Yes!"

"What about robots? Have you got any robots on board?"

"No robots or bananas. It is cutting-edge: robots attacking bananas…that is real cutting-edge, sir."

"Is it?"

"Of course!"

George groaned as he remembered back in the day, more than two hundred years ago, how much he had embraced science and technology, and just how moronic it had become; and perhaps felt some guilt for his promotion of the sciences. He looked at his hands.

"Our hands!" he said. "They are part of our human body. Would they see our hands?"

"You are right, sir; they would definitely see our hands. We must cover them."

Figgis rushed off to a little cupboard and came back with four brown paper bags."

"Paper bags?"

"Yes. As soon as we land, you must cover your hands with the bags. Cover them so the robots cannot see your hands. We are coming in to land now."

Figgis rushed back to the cockpit to bring the plane down.

The engines screeched, and George William tensed up, fearing the two million robots would react, and covered his hands with his two paper bags.

The plane hit the ground, throwing up a mountain of dust. Surely the robots must be alerted? Figgis swung the plane around near to the secret entrance to the fortress. He opened the aircraft door and covered his hands.

"Come on, sir, we only have forty-five seconds to get into the fortress."

Figgis rushed out of the plane. George William followed.

After being in the plane the desert was scorchingly dry and blindingly bright, and George was supremely nervous of the two million robots lying in wait among the hissing scorpions.

"Hurry along, sir!" Figgis urged.

George rushed along, keeping his hands upright so the bags would not fall off: four ridiculous brown paper bags rushing towards the entrance, which was a rock. The rock opened as they approached, and Figgis pushed George William inside.

"We are in!" Figgis said.

The rock snapped closed.

George William was relieved.

2

Inside the fortress, it was dark after the brightness of the desert, and cooler too.

George William asked. "Is it safe to take off the paper bags now?"

"Yes, I think so."

Figgis took his bags off, so George William did the same.

Figgis tore down the corridor with a new sense of purpose. George William followed. "Where are we going? This is not where we put the trunk."

"I want to see my invention one last time. My control centre that controlled all our robot bases around the Earth; the control centre we had to abandon because of Mr Zakamonsky. I want to see it one last time."

Figgis rushed down the dark, rock-lined corridors towards the staircase that led all the way down into the robot command centre. They reached the stairway and began the descent into its great command hall.

The great hall was a huge cave filled with electronic equipment, and as they dropped down, the hall lit up like some wonderland of electronic gadgetry. Figgis hummed with pride.

"My control room: the hub of our world-wide army! Taken thirty years for me to build this! I shall reactivate for one last look; activate for a few minutes, no longer. Just a few minutes, in case Mr Zakamonsky's robots outside decide to storm the fortress and succeed."

"George William became alert. "Is that likely? Could they storm the fortress while we are inside?"

"It is possible. It was always likely they would invade the fortress. That is why we left. I am surprised they have not stormed it up till now. It is why I deactivated the control centre. A disaster would befall the Earth if Mr Zakamonsky discovered the secrets of the control centre; it would surely be the end! It is bad enough Mr Zakamonsky having taken the Mojave base. With

Mr Zakamonsky having control of the whole system, it would be the finish. He could take over the Earth within hours. Two hundred million robot soldiers at strategic bases across the globe, primed for the job. It would be over very quickly. There would be no way back."

"Then we must make sure that will not happen," George said, grimly.

"That is why I shall reactivate for a few minutes only."

"Will they know if the system has been reactivated?"

"At some point, yes. I do not know how long it will take. Obviously, if they knew the system was active, they would storm the fortress right away."

"With us inside?"

"Yes, particularly with us inside! It would give them the opportunity to torture us and get us to reveal all the secrets."

"I thought they could not see us."

"They could see our hands. They could bend our fingers backwards, even snap them off, until we revealed the secrets."

George William recoiled and rapidly re-covered his hands with the paper bags. "Are you sure they cannot see through these paper bags?"

"I do not think so."

"What do you mean 'I do not think so'? If you say something, you must be certain about it; if you are not certain, don't say it. Is that clear?"

"Yes, all right."

They reached the bottom of the staircase and were in the Great Hall. It was alive with the electrotonic hum of technology. “Why are we taking the risk of reactivating the system? Why are we doing this?”

Figgis was melancholy. “I want to see the system one last time: thirty years’ work. It is the most advanced system the world has ever seen – and I made it! One final look at my creation, it is a brilliant creation. I want one last look.”

“Very well, make it quick!”

They advanced to the master control desk and took their seats – two seats, one for Figgis one for George William – and were engulfed by a large, semi-circular assemblance of two hundred screens: one screen for every base around the Earth. In the middle, a larger screen for the Head of all Head robots; the big screen, for Chief Robot Robert. Off to one side was the screen of the Mojave base, sadly taped up with a notice: *‘Now under Mr Zakamonsky’s control.’*

George William surveyed the array of screens, melancholy too, remembering the time, just over three months previously; the time he sat alone in this hall, in this chair surrounded by the two hundred screens. Bases in every corner of the globe, each manned by millions of robots soldiers, instantly available to carry out every command ordered of them. How he wished he had had it in his own day, but now it was available to him: the most fantastic military system every devised; now all ruined by leaving one base unsecured and letting Zakamonsky hack into it.

Figgis pressed a button and Chief Robot Robert came up on the main screen.

“Chief Robert, this is Aloysius Figgis speaking. You will only be able to view my hands in this instance.”

“I recognise those hands, Esteemed Founder.”

“Robert, please activate the bowing protocol throughout the remaining bases across the Earth.”

The Chief Robot bowed and said, “Yes, Your Esteemed Highness! I will enact bowing protocols throughout the remaining bases. One moment please.” A few seconds elapsed. “Yes, it is ready for you now.”

Figgis flicked another button and the remaining bases, another one hundred and ninety-eight of them, came to life, each base with their own screen. Head robots from across the globe: muscular, decorated strongmen flanked by hundreds of thousands of their foot soldiers. The decorated strongmen bowed respectfully before their founder, then in one huge wave the millions of foot soldiers behind them began bowing too. Figgis basked in the glory: tens of millions of robot soldiers bowing to him in the huge arc of screens surrounding him. Figgis was absolutely luxuriating in it. Then, they started jumping in ecstasy. “Aloysius, Aloysius, Aloysius!” They shouted, and did it again. “Aloysius! Aloysius! Aloysius! Aloysius!” they kept repeating.

“Why are they doing that, Figgis?”

Figgis turned to him sourly. “You never call me by my first name. I have never heard you once calling me by my first name. I like being called by my first name.”

George William was pained. “You must understand that a man in my position cannot call you by your first name.” He said it almost pleadingly: “It is simply not decent for a man in my position to do this. You understand that; surely you can understand, can’t you?”

“No.”

Figgis looked away, and on the screens the millions of robots shouted louder. “Aloysius! Aloysius! Aloysius! Aloysius the Magnificent!” they shouted. They continued shouting for another couple of minutes.

“That is most gratifying, Robert. Thank you, they can stop now. I would like you to do something else: design me a robot. A robot that looks half-human and half-gorilla. Big, fifteen feet tall. Big roar!”

“Will do, Your Esteemed Highness,” Robert said.

“Good man, Robert. It will have a special function.” He typed instructions in for the special function of this robot, then closed the system down.

Figgis said glumly to George William: “Come on, sir, let us retrieve the white stone.”

There was a faint rumble from upstairs.

3

The trunk had been placed in a store room on an upper level of the fortress. The store room, another cave, was dim and musky. The trunk was huge; like some over-sized buccaneer's chest. It had studs, metal rivets and straps. Big leather straps secured tight with big brass buckles that had become mouldy.

"Good. We've found the trunk. Figgis, get the thing open!"

Figgis inspected the trunk, and the straps in particular. "I cannot do it on my own; the straps are tough. I need your help. I need your hands to assist me."

George protectively clasped his hands together, holding the paper bags in place. "What about the robots? What if they come in and see my hands?"

"Do you want to get the white stone or not?"

"Of course we need the white stone."

"Then get those bags off and help me!"

George reluctantly removed the paper bags. "Let's make this quick. What do you want me to do?"

"You release the buckle while I pull the strap."

"I release the buckle while you pull the strap?"

"That's right, sir."

George William got his hands on the buckle and Figgis pulled the strap. The buckle lifted half an inch and George William wedged his fingers behind it.

George said. "You need get the buckle up a bit more so I can push the pin through the hole in the strap. You need to pull it harder."

"I am already pulling it hard."

"Put more gumption in it man– pull it harder!"

Figgis huffed and puffed and pulled. The strap did not move. He gave a giant tug and fell backwards as the strap snapped. "Ow!" The buckle snapped down, trapping George's fingers. "Oh, this is bloody marvellous," George William growled.

Figgis got up and inspected the strap. "It has snapped just below the buckle. There is nothing left to pull. Nothing."

"Well, get a knife or a saw. My fingers are now trapped."

"Where do I find a knife?"

"I don't know – the girls' kitchen, probably."

There was another rumble; louder, a bit like some pneumatic drill boring through the rock.

George said nervously: "What is that?"

"Not sure, sir. Sounds like drilling."

"Get that damned knife quickly."

Figgis found a long, sharp knife in the kitchen and brought it back. The drilling sounds had stopped.

"Cut the strap above the buckle…and be careful of my fingers. This buckle is old and rusty, it may need some oil."

Figgis cut the strap, successfully, and together they managed (without oil) to release George's fingers from the buckle. George was relieved and began to nurse his fingers.

"What do you think that drilling was? Is it the robots drilling into the fortress?"

"Yes, it could be," Figgis said, and had a think.

After George had nursed his fingers, he quickly put the paper bags protectively over his hands.

Figgis had a think and piped up: "It is not the robots. It is the aliens!"

"What do you mean?"

"You remember just over three months ago when Mr Zakamonsky first tried to invade our base with his band of aliens?"

"Oh, yes. The advance party of aliens that were living in the old sewers of Gdansk."

"That's right, sir. He sent over one hundred of them to invade our fortress. We captured them and locked them up. They started drilling through the cells so I got the robots to seal them in with a hundred yards of concrete."

"Oh yes, forgot about that."

"They must have been drilling for over three months. They are probably reaching the end of our wall of cement." The drilling sound became louder. "They could emerge any moment. They will be very angry."

"Oh Lord, this is a terrible situation. We have a hundred aliens who are going to really take it out on us for the way we so cruelly locked them up; and we have two million robots outside, who want to capture us, and probably torture us until we tell the secrets of the control room." He looked at the paper bags covering his hands. "Would the aliens see the paper bags?"

"The aliens are not blind. I imagine they would see them. Frankly, I don't think it would make much difference whether you had the bags on your hands or not."

George was in a quandary here, and a large amount of a panic.

Figgis was getting itchy. "Come on, sir; I don't fancy hanging around. What do you want to do?"

George William thought for a few seconds. "We must do what we came here to do; get this trunk opened and retrieve the white stone!"

"Are sure about that?"

"Yes."

"Are you going to help?"

"Yes."

Together, they dealt with the straps and opened the trunk, limited as their capabilities were; each pair of hands at either end of the trunk. The lid was stiff, it squeaked and creaked like some horror movie. It creaked it's way until it was fully opened.

The trunk opened up like an ancient treasure trove. Tens of thousands of drawings on old paper; thousands bound together and tied with ribbons.

"What is all this, sir?"

"Drawings and inventions by the original George Tipton. He was a great artist."

"Fascinating. I would like to have a look at some of these, sir."

"Not now, Figgis, we need to act fast. We need to find the white stone and somehow get out of here."

As if to emphasise the urgency, the drilling started up once again.

"What does the white stone look like?"

"I imagine it is a stone that is white. If you search the bottom of the trunk, I will search the top."

"Right-oh, sir."

Figgis climbed in and very soon disappeared under piles of drawings, and began burrowing underground like a rabbit.

"It is very dark in here, sir."

"Just get on with it, Figgis."

While Figgis burrowed below, George sifted up top. The drilling got louder. It was just a few feet above them on the next level, and seemed like they could break through the concrete at any moment.

"Hurry up, Figgis – we need to find that stone and evacuate!"

"I think I have found something."

"Is it the white stone?"

"No, it is a box."

"Is the stone inside the box?

"I don't know."

"Bring it up."

Figgis burrowed up and presented a box. A velvety box.

George opened it. The white stone - it was there! A wonderful, shimmering, round piece of white perfection.

"We got it. We must ensure the aliens do not get it." The drilling was getting louder. "How are we going to get out of here?"

"How do you fancy being a pigeon?"

"Not very much."

"Have you ever been a pigeon, sir?"

"Of course I have never been a pigeon. What kind of stupid question is that?"

Figgis smiled and whistled. The two, fifteen-foot gorilla robots he'd ordered Robert to manufacture, arrived. They were big hairy beasts that looked half-human, half-gorilla.

“I have programmed the DNA of pigeons into them. They can turn us into pigeons and we can make our escape. ”

“I don’t want to be a pigeon.”

“I know of a passage to the desert outside. A hole. We could fly through it undetected. As pigeons.”

“What about the stone? We have to rescue the girls.”

“We could carry the stone in our beaks. You could carry it in your beak. We would fly to them and deliver it. You can drop it into Georgina’s hands.”

“I don’t want to be a pigeon. I have things to do. I am meant to be ruling the world.”

“No sir. I think we have had enough of this world. Too complicated and dangerous. Two little pigeons. Flying side by side. Not a care in the world. What could be nicer?”

“Figgis, this is ridiculous.”

“We could continue our adventures in the bird world.”

“I do not want to have adventures in the bird world. I have things to do in this world.”

“It would be good for our relationship.”

“George William said. “What relationship is that, Figgis?”

“It would be good for us. You’ll see. We will have a whole new outlook on life. In any case we haven’t got any other option. If the aliens don’t get us, the robots will.”

George was becoming frantic. “If we do become pigeons, once this is over, can you get me back to the human world?”

“I don’t know. I am not sure. Not sure if that is possible, but it is the right thing to do. The only thing we can do. Look on the bright side, it might be fun.”

“Fun, fun?”

“We shall continue working together in birdworld!”

Figgis became suddenly masterful. He instructed the gorilla robots. “We wish to become pigeons,” he said to them. “We shall continue our existence in pigeon world! Initiate the Pigeon DNA protocols on us now! Do it immediately!” Figgis ordered.

4

Fredrick said, “Oh dear. George William ending up as a pigeon. I didn’t see that one coming.”

Hubert asked, “Would George William carry on his mission as a pigeon?”

“I do not know; I am not sure if he can.”

“Could he rule the world as a pigeon? Could a pigeon rule the world?”

“Of all the scenarios, I did not factor in that one. Unless George William comes up with some miracle as a pigeon, I think we had better scrub George William out of the equation. George William a pigeon, oh dear! That just leaves Georgina Tipton and Mr Zakamonsky. Unless

Georgina can overcome Zakamonsky, it just leaves him. The one we did not want: Zakamonsky. It is not looking good."

Hubert said. "We could always watch and see how George William gets on in bird-world."

"Not now Hubert. We need to see what Georgina Tipton is doing. Come on, let's hover over."

CHAPTER EIGHT

1

Georgina was broken. Fooled and trapped on an endless trip around the Earth, distressed and heartbroken. Slouched on top of her barge, around and around the Earth she went, disillusioned and tired; her illusions of being someone special, gone. Slumped in her seat, she watched years and years go by; years of human degradation. She did not even bother trying to be a Goddess. Everything pointless: Zakamonsky had won. He had fooled her like her had fooled everyone else. All she could do was acquiesce, like everyone else, and look on as he triumphed; triumphed in a pool of human misery.

The rebellion had passed years ago. They had succumbed. Populations worldwide had gone through many of phases of humiliation. Currently, they were living a Stone Age existence: an outdoor life huddled together in fields and caves, some on river banks; clustered around campfires, trying to keep warm; praising Zakamonsky; praying to him.

"Thank you Mr Zakamonsky for our daily bread," they prayed.

The chanted this everywhere. In the caves, they chanted: "Thank you Mr Zakamonsky for our daily bread. Thank you for our cave."

It was not just humans who were doing this; it was his own people, too. "Thank you Mr Zakamonsky for our daily bread, thank you very much," they chanted. They too, like humans, were living primitive, outdoor lives. "Thank you Mr Zakamonsky for our daily bread, thank you for bringing us to this wonderful land," they chanted, shivering. Around the world little groups congregated around fires chanting the same thing.

Yes; Zakamonsky had fooled everyone, even his own people, his victory total, his domination complete. Everyone was worshiping Zakamonsky, and Georgina was forced to witness it. Defeated, disillusioned, she too was finally broken. She pushed out a prayer of her own.

"You have won Mr Zakamonsky. I acknowledge your victory. Please have mercy on us and let us go. If you have an ounce of compassion in you, as I thought you did, you will let us go."

Bawling away, Zakamonsky appeared.

"Why are you weeping, my dear?"

"You have won. Everyone is worshipping you as you wanted."

"I could change that. I could have them saying *'Thank you Mr Zakamonsky and the Goddess Georgina for our daily bread.'* I could even have you put in front. '*Thank you Goddess Georgina and Zakamonsky for our daily bread.'* We could do it that way if you want."

"What?"

"You and me running the Earth. We are in this together aren't we?"

"Are we? It is all you, all your plan. None mine! I do not want populations living outside, thanking us for their horrible conditions."

"I am working towards the final outcome; populations have to be conditioned for the final outcome. Humans, also my people, have to be conditioned. You have to see the final outcome; it is fantastic!"

"It is not right, Mr Zakamonsky."

"Just wait for the final outcome. Be patient!"

"Show me the final outcome," Georgina demanded.

"You are disrupting my presentation," Zakamonsky said. "You will miss out on all the finesse I have put into this programme: the painstaking rehabilitation of our two peoples."

"I want to see the final outcome," Georgina insisted.

Zakamonsky was disappointed. "If you must," he said. "Fine. Get ready to experience the final outcome!"

The theatre went completely black.

Two minutes later, everything came alive once more – a full two hundred years in the future. Georgina and Charlotte had aged. Zakamonsky had been true to his word and given them five hundred extra years of life, but they had aged, aged into early middle-age; the girls' faces had matured. Squires's fingers had matured too. They remained on the barge and it was sailing down the Ohio River. They came to a bend in the river. Ahead, an island. They sailed to the right side of the island, and Charlotte came out of her comatose state.

"There is something familiar about this," Charlotte said.

Zakamonsky nodded.

Charlotte asked "Is it Brunot Island?"

Zakamonsky smiled. "It is! You have come home. After two hundred years, I have brought you home. Come with me and look!"

Like Mary Poppins, the whole party floated up from the river: up, up and away from the barge, up to Pennsylvania Heights; a suburban enclave of Pittsburgh, the district Georgina and Charlotte had lived in for most of their lives. They floated over the few streets of their neighbourhood. Proud sturdy houses in their own plots, gardens front and back, built in the early 1900's. It was a heritage neighbourhood when they lived in it; now three hundred years old, it was proper heritage. The neighbourhood had aged gracefully and been perfectly preserved.

"I have kept the whole of your early patch intact," Zakamonsky said, proudly.

They landed in the garden of Charlotte's house.

"Your garden, your house – everything preserved as it was: not quite. I have added much ancient foliage and flowers; foliage and flowers that had become extinct. I have brought them back; returned to life the best flowers and foliage from the last few thousand years, and now that humans will no longer destroy them, they are able to flourish. Isn't that good?"

"This is amazing, Mr Zakamonsky," Charlotte said; agog. Right in the middle of her garden two hundred years in the future. The beauty was astounding; surreal; like some mythical garden come alive.

Zakamonsky proudly took them on tour of the garden, pointing out various previously extinct vegetation. "Your house and garden is in a better condition than the one you left. I have kept it in your honour; tended by a rota of families. It is a great privilege to look after your house. Step back a little: the family should be coming out any moment to give thanks for this great honour. We shall see them, and then move on to observe how humans are now living; living in perfect harmony. No wars: perfect respect. We shall see them next. Here comes the family!"

A mother and two children emerged: a stunningly beautiful family who were dizzying to look at in their perfection.

"Children, give thanks for the opportunity to look after the ancestral home." the mother said.

The children approached a little shrine and began their praise.

"Thank you for the opportunity to look after the house. Thank you Goddess Georgina for being in our lives. May you always be in our lives. We pray for you to stay in our lives forever."

"Now give thanks to the Goddess Georgina's cousin, Charlotte. Pray that she can one day become a Goddess too."

"We pray the Goddess's cousin will do the sensible thing and one day become a Goddess too."

The mother said, "Now give thanks to the family's guardian."

The children opened their arms and said, "Thank you, Mr Squires, for being the family's guardian. Bless you, Mr Squires!"

Squires took a double flip and approached Zakamonsky. "They are blessing me for being the family's guardian!"

"Yes, Mr Squires. You have the position of protector of the Earth's First Family."

"Protector of the Earth's First Family? That is very good of you, Mr Zakamonsky," Squires said

"You are welcome. Now go away while I talk with the Goddess Georgina."

Zakamonsky addressed Georgina. "What do you think, my dear? A good outcome?"

Georgina was puzzled. "What about the two hundred years of pain?"

"Regrettably, a necessary step in reaching the final outcome. Let me show you how humans are now living; how humans are working together in harmony. You will be impressed."

"No," Georgina said. "I want to discuss the two hundred years of pain."

"Wait until you see how people are living, and you will see it has all been worth it."

"No!" Georgina demanded. "Stop this presentation! We need to discuss this two hundred years of pain. We need to discuss it now!"

Zakamonsky was upset, but stopped the presentation. The cinema returned to normal. Everyone blinked as they realised they were still in their plush, velvety seats. It had been a very realistic presentation.

"What do you want to discuss?" Zakamonsky asked sourly.

"Two hundred years of pain is not right."

"In my experience, you have to tell people over and over before they get the point: many generations. Two to three lifetimes at least. By the time the fifth or sixth generation come along they should get the point. I had wanted to do two or three thousand years for my people, but I only have five hundred years left. I am becoming an old man, Gina."

"You are a cruel man, Mr Zakamonsky."

Zakamonsky was hurt. "Then tell me how you would do it? How would you manage the transition period?"

Georgina thought, and went a little blank.

"See – I knew you would not know. Just let me handle the nasties and we can rule together afterwards."

"No, wait!" she felt the stone in her purse and took it out. Her stone was still in Zakamonsky's realm. "My stone would hold the answer. If the stone was back in the Earth realm, I would know the answer. I will tell you how to manage the transition if you turn the stone back into the Earth realm!"

"You think the stone could tell you that?"

"Yes. If my stone was back in the Earth realm, I am certain it could! All of the glorious secrets of the Earth realm are contained in the stone. The way forward for the Earth would be revealed in the stone…if it was back in the Earth realm."

Zakamonsky looked worried. More than that: he was gaping into space as if he was no longer there.

Georgina looked at him, puzzled. "What is the matter?"

Zakamonsky did not answer; he was in some other place, and looking like some terrified child. "I forgot," he said finally.

"What did you forget?"

Zakamonsky took his stone out from his cape and stared at it, becoming adrift in some deep, lost memory. "I had forgotten what the stone was for." Zakamonsky said absorbed in a long-forgotten past. "It is bringing up memories: long-forgotten memories."

"What memories?"

"Can I trust you?"

"Trust me with what?"

"My memories."

Georgina nodded. "Yes, I will not tell anyone."

"Not about revealing them; it is about abusing me. Can I trust you?"

He looked at her with his little-boy eyes and Georgina was shocked to see a hurt, innocent little boy: a terrified little boy.

She touched his arm. "Tell me about it," she said.

"Can I trust you?"

"You can tell me, but if you feel uncomfortable, then stop."

"Hmmm," he said. "Your touch feels soothing. I hope I can trust you."

"You can, and you can stop if it feels uncomfortable."

Zakamonsky led them off to seats on the third row.

2

Sitting next to Georgina on the third row, Zakamonsky looked at his stone and reminisced. "I was presented with this stone at an extremely early age: a young child. Barely any experience of living. Maybe I had reached the age of four in Earthly years."

Georgina nodded. "That is a young age to receive the stone."

"As heir apparent of my realm, I was given the stone by the keepers. I do not know why, but I had become the chosen one. The keepers, three of them, came to my bedroom in my father's house and whisked me off to the Imperial Palace many miles away. It was the most happy and magical experience of my entire life."

He paused for a while as he thought through this magical memory, and he shone with a simple joy.

"The keepers took me to the secret anointing room. Even the current ruler of the time did not know it was there. They anointed me with this very stone." He turned the stone over, inspecting it closely. "The Keepers said the stone would give me the power and wisdom to rule the realm, and I was the one chosen to do it. The stone would only give me the power to do this when I was one hundred years. That is about ten Earthly years: still a child. Until I was of age, I must keep the stone with me and never let it out of my sight."

"That is a long time to keep the stone safe without it having any power."

"I think you understand," Zakamonsky said smiling. "The keepers told me my core mission was to bring my people back through redemption. My realm is a wild place, full of dangerous people; a realm of the fallen. Many have fallen from a situation of supreme grace – a long fall. My role as ruler was to rehabilitate my people and return them to a position of grace. The keepers told me the stone would show me the path of this redemption; the stone would give me the wisdom to rehabilitate my people."

"I knew it! I knew your stone would be able to do that!"

"You could be right. The keepers delivered me back to my bedroom in my father's house. They repeated I should never let the stone out of my sight. It was like some wonderful, magical dream, but it was not a dream. In the morning, I woke up with the stone and knew I had to keep it safe; safe until I became of age. The early years were happy. No one knew it was there. I slept with the stone. Then someone did find out about the stone."

"Oh."

Zakamonsky's light demeanour darkened. "It is a painful story. Extremely painful."

Georgina touched his arm. "Tell me. I want to hear the story of you and your stone."

"A brutal man from Earth tried to steal the stone from me. He had found out about the stone and the power it had. He knew I had it. A human tried to steal my stone! He was determined to steal it by whatever means so that he could be the ruler of the realm. I was older, but still a young child. He followed me from school and chased me into the forest. I clutched my stone, but he caught me. He shook me and held me in a vice-like grip. He searched my body. Before he found the stone, I managed to extract it and get it in my mouth and swallowed it. This was very painful. He became angry and beat me. He took me to a room and locked me in it. He waited until I excreted the stone. For three days, I managed to keep it inside. He became impatient and sent for a surgeon to cut me open. I managed to escape; through a long, dark shaft I escaped. It took me ten days of hunger and hiding to find my way home. When I arrived, my father beat me; he beat me and beat me. That was the start of my affliction."

"Affliction?"

"The start of the process that turned me psychotic. A long catalogue of torture went on throughout my childhood. It is too painful and I do not want to talk about it now."

"No, some other time." Georgina said.

"Now I have told you I am a psychotic, I suppose it is over between us?

"Not necessarily; you have been honest."

"I had brutal teachers and a brutal father. The whole of my realm was brutal. Post-apocalypse brutality. Everyone was brutal. I became hardened and brutal, too. I managed to keep the stone with me until I became of age; kept it intact through a very long period of attacks."

"That is a great achievement," Georgina said.

"Thank you. Once I became of age, the stone gave me the ability to take control of my people and rule them. I did this, and restored order to the realm. I ruled harshly but order was maintained, and since that time there has never been any trouble. My people obey me completely." He smiled a little with the pride of this achievement. "Although I was slow to start my core mission, I never completely forgot it."

"The redemption of your people?"

"Yes. Maybe I should tell you about my people?"

"Yes, do tell me about them."

"They are beautiful super-race: a race beyond humans; an earlier race. They have fallen, fallen extremely far. From beautiful, immaculate beings down to giant slugs. Huge slugs with just a little of what appears to be human peeping out; humans peeping through their eyes and mouth. Once they have worked their way up, they gradually appear more human. Their true state though, is way past human: an intelligent super-race that has fallen. Fallen after the apocalypse long back; before known human history began. Some were instrumental in the apocalypse. Most were complicit. Their only way back is through redemption. The keepers charged me with their redemption."

Georgina tried to assimilate this revelation. "So your people are a beautiful super-race that existed before known human history?"

"Yes."

"And they live in a misty-red realm mainly as giant slugs waiting for redemption?"

"Yes. I never forget my main mission, but what I did forget was using the stone to achieve it."

He paused to regain his thoughts, then carried on: "Six-hundred years ago, I started on my core mission: rehabilitation of my people. In a moment of vision, I saw how to achieve this. I need to mention, it was my vision, and not that of the stone. I thought if my people could come to Earth, be in the beauty of the Earth, I could begin to rehabilitate them in the earthly environment. My people long for the Earth; are engrained with countless images of it; pine for it, but know it is an unobtainable, evaporated dream. Well, I would make it attainable for them! Give them hope and a goal – also a tool to maintain order over them. I trained up two hundred men to come to Earth as an expeditionary force. It was a big mission that could take up to eight hundred years. In the 1500's, they landed in the northern forests near the Baltic coast. It took them one hundred years to adapt to human appearance and mannerisms. Their mission was to secure lands for a few thousand of my people to be rehabilitated in. After the first lot were done, I would rehabilitate the next lot, and so on. This was my plan. My field commander took on the name of Albrecht and the whole brigade settled in the town of Danzig. Here, they formed themselves into a crack security unit designed to carry out special operations. They got taken on as an independent wing of the Prussian Army. During this time they came into contact with an ancestor of George William. This man was aiming to become The Holy Roman Emperor of the time, with nearly a whole continent at his disposal. My field Commander Albrecht offered the man exclusive use of his crack security force in exchange for some lands. The man agreed."

"What happened then?"

"He betrayed me. He betrayed me! That human betrayed me! Another human betrayed me!" Zakamonsky was starting to go psychotic, simply by thinking about it. Georgina reached out and touched his shoulder. "Calm down," she said. "That was all a long time ago."

Zakamonsky recovered a minute later. "Thank you, thank you! I think I have just discovered a small touch of affection can cure a bout of my psychosis."

"Just a small touch? Is that all it needs?"

"Yes, amazing isn't it?"

"I would say!"

"No one has ever touched me before. Nobody has ever given me affection."

"I am glad to help. So how did George William's ancestor betray you?"

"Please do not remind me. No! No! No! - He betrayed me! Not do what he promised! Betrayed me! Betrayal, that is what it was! Outright act of betrayal!!" Zakamonsky started to panic and slipping into an angry psychosis. Georgina frantically touched him with both bands; touched his head and chest using both hands. After a minute or two he recovered.

"Ah, that is much better, thank you."

"We had better stay off the subject of George William's ancestor."

"Yes."

"It is really good I am able to cure you."

"Yes."

"I am happy to be able to cure you; it feels good to help people."

"Does it feel good?" Zakamonsky was curious.

"Yes. I think you need to go on a course of what feels good, as you only seem to know what feels bad A 'feel-good' course."

"A 'feel-good' course? Yes, perhaps that is what I need. Do you provide feel-good courses?

"No."

"How do I get on a feel-good course?"

Georgina was regretting she mentioned this. "I will give you some pointers," she said. "I shall try to point out what feels good, and what does not."

"That will be very nice. Thank you."

"Now let us talk about the stones. My stone and your stone." Georgina remembered her main aim was getting her stone back to where it should be. "Let us talk stones!"

Zakamonsky turned mournful. "Yes, after four and a half thousand years you have reminded me. Woken me up to what I should done four thousand years ago. If only I had consulted my stone four thousand years ago. All things that have gone wrong in the last four thousand years are down to me. It could have been so different." He was regretful, bereft, the full weight of his responsibility weighing down on him.

Georgina stopped him: forcefully snapping, "Now is the time to put it right! Consult your stone now and discover the way to put it right!"

Zakamonsky looked at her making a dramatic change. "You are very right; I must do it now." He immediately diverted his eyes to gaze at his stone, gazed deeply.

"And I should consult mine. Together, we could consult them for the best outcome."

"Yes, the two stones together. Nobody has ever done that before. That is an amazing idea!" Zakamonsky dived in to contemplate on his stone with intensity.

Georgina said, "The trouble is, I cannot consult my stone because it is in your realm." Zakamonsky did not hear this because of the deepness of his contemplation.

He concentrated hard, and a transformation came over him. An aura formed. A beautiful aura surrounding his body. Georgina, although frustrated, watched, intrigued.

Zakamonsky looked up from his stone. "It is beginning to reveal the form of redemption my people should take."

"What is it?"

"It is revealing my people should serve humans with humility; without any hint of superiority."

"What service should your people perform for humans?"

"That is still to be revealed." Zakamonsky returned to contemplating with the stone, and a little while later he looked up, "It is your stone that will reveal the service my people must perform. It is as you suggested. Our two stones working side-by-side. Why are you not consulting your stone?"

"I cannot!" Georgina showed him her stone. "I cannot, because my stone is in your realm!"

"We must get it back into your realm."

"Can you do that? Can you get my stone back into the Earth realm?"

"We must! The wisdom of the two realms must be working together, side-by-side!"

"You can get my stone back into the Earth realm? In the Earth realm on full power?"

"Yes! We must! Come with me!"

Georgina became curiously excited.

Zakamonsky took Georgina to a booth at the rear of the cinema.

3

The booth was a communication hub into Zakamonsky's laboratory underneath his palace. Designed by his own scientists it had a direct connection to his wizened old Chief Scientist, who sat, as he always did, in the reddish haze, on his little throne in the middle of the great laboratory hall. The Chief Scientist realising he was in the presence of the Supreme Commander, bowed. "It is an honour once again to be in your presence," he said.

"Chief Scientist, I have to inform you there has been a significant change in my plans; instead, our people are going to unite with the Earth people to form a bright new chapter in the history of the universe!"

"That is wonderful news, Supreme Commander. A wonderful thing to for us to do!"

"There is one obstacle we need to overcome. I am in possession of the mighty stone of our realm, but the mighty stone of the Earth realm has become corrupted. We need to restore the Earth stone to its true state."

"On full power." Georgina added.

"Repair and restore the Earth stone on full power." Zakamonsky said.

"This will be a great honour and great challenge," the wizened old scientist said. "Working out the composition of the Earth stone, repairing it, and transmitting this information to the Earth, and into the stone. A great challenge."

Zakamonsky said, "I may be able to help. With the assistance of the great stone of our realm, I have been trawling through my memory and realised the secret codes of every realm of the stone are held in our own ancient vaults. They were placed there dozens of millennia ago. The composition of the Earth stone is in the sacred ancient vaults of our own realm!"

"I have heard of these ancient sacred vaults, but where are they?"

"Below you: deep below the great laboratory hall are the ancient vaults."

The Chief Scientist looked down. "I did not know there were other halls beneath this hall."

"Oh yes: the halls have not been in use for a long long time; halls of great knowledge that have been sealed for many millennia. In amongst these halls is the secret passage to the ancient vault of our realm. It has not been visited for four and a half thousand years."

"Four and a half thousand years? Near the beginning of your reign, Supreme Commander?"

"Not near – at the start of my reign. It was at this time the keepers retrieved the great stone of our realm from the vault; retrieved it and anointed me with it. That is the last time the vault was opened."

"Thank you for telling me this, Supreme Commander."

"As a very young child, the keepers anointed me as the saviour of this realm; said that I should regard the great stone as my sceptre, for it holds the wisdom and route to the redemption of our realm. It will show us the way back to the promised land. This is what I have been anointed to do."

The Chief Scientist, who looked ninety-five per cent human, suddenly went up a notch to ninety-six per cent, and bowed his head in awe. "This is what I want, Supreme Commander. This is what I have always wanted: the promised land! This is what all of our people want!"

"I shall tell you now: the promised land will be achieved in conjunction with the Earth realm. It will be achieved in concurrence with the wisdom from the great stone of the Earth. Organise a party to enter the ancient vault so we may retrieve the codes for the great stone of the Earth."

"I will do this immediately," the wizened old scientist said, with growing excitement. "How do we enter the ancient vaults? Where is the entrance?"

"I will contemplate with the great stone of our realm to seek guidance. In the meantime, organise a party of two to assemble at the far end of the laboratory hall and await my instructions. One should be an expert in ancient cyphers; the other have an agile body. Both must be willing to be manipulated by the grace of the stone."

"Yes, Supreme Commander! Thank you!" The Chief Scientist got to work organising the party.

In the booth, Zakamonsky began contemplating with the stone pressing the bright jewel against his forehead. He went into a deep trance and his body glowed. Georgina was in wonder. A few minutes later, the Chief Scientist informed him the party had gathered.

"Tell your party to stand away from the wall!" Zakamonsky ordered.

The men were instructed. The floor opened up revealing a passage leading to a steep downward corridor carved out of rock. "Men enter into the corridor and make great haste," Zakamonsky told them.

The men rushed down into the corridor. "You are the first ones to enter this most-secret area in four and a half thousand years," Zakamonsky said to them. "Hurry, for the area will shut down in four and a half minutes. It is uncertain when it shall re-open." The men bolted down the passage. Zakamonsky went on: "Thirty seconds ahead is a junction with many tunnels leading to the lower levels. You must take the fifth tunnel to the east." Seconds later, they reached the junction and the men took the fifth tunnel to the east. They hurried as the tunnel dropped down a level, then widened and became carpeted, golden, and adorned with ornaments. Very soon, the tunnel ended and the ancient vault was before them. To one side a rock; carved into it was the ancient cypher. "Run your hands over the ancient encryption," Zakamonsky said to the cypher man, "assimilate the information, and surrender your mind and body to me."

The cypher man ran his hands over the ancient cypher calculating its meaning, and with great effort let his mind and body go limp for Zakamonsky. Zakamonsky took control and the man's hand, like some manic chimpanzee, rapidly tapped different rocks in sequence. The great door of the vault opened; the light inside was blinding. Zakamonsky switched to the other man. "Shield your eyes. Let your body go limp and I will guide it to the ancient formula of the Earth Stone. Keep your eyes closed, for the light will blind you!" With great effort, the man's body went limp and he closed his eyes placing one hand over them too. Zakamonsky manipulated him into the light. A few yards inside the vault he stopped at a shelf, and with the other hand extracted a document. Zakamonsky manipulated the man back and out of the vault. The great door closed.

"Hurry back to the laboratory hall and deliver the document to the Chief Scientist." Zakamonsky ordered.

The men rushed back up the tunnel, and Zakamonsky withdrew the stone from his forehead; depleted, but elated.

The men reached the great laboratory a full thirty seconds before the floor closed up. They rushed to deliver the document to the Chief Scientist. The Chief Scientist read through the documents with great excitement.

"Are they the correct documents?" Zakamonsky asked.

"Indeed they are, Supreme Commander."

"How long to transmit the information to the Earth stone and reinstate it?"

The Chief Scientist's head began to throb then expand as he worked out the complexities of doing this. "Two to three weeks," he said finally.

Zakamonsky shook his head. "No – this must be done immediately! Within an hour or two the Earth stone must be reinstated and active. Turn over the entire hall to work on this!"

The Chief Scientist looked up and down the vast hall. Two and a half thousand scientists were working to his left; two and a half thousand scientists to his right. All working diligently in the red, hazy mist. The Chief Scientist used his superior brain to sequence work on the job and organise groups of one hundred scientists; each group to work on an element of the task. "I shall turn over the entire hall to work on this. The work should take two to three hours; it cannot be done quicker," the Chief Scientist said.

Zakamonsky said, "That will be fine. Contact me know when it is ready."

"Yes, Supreme Commander," the scientist was greatly relieved. "Thank you, thank you. Historic day!"

"Yes, historic day." Zakamonsky said smiling.

Georgina was in awe of what had just happened, not least because she was about to receive her stone.

4

Leaving the booth, Georgina blinked. "I am in awe! You really understand your stone, don't you?"

"That was simple stuff. You have not seen anything yet!"

Georgina was chilled with excitement. "I cannot wait until my stone is ready! You working your stone, me working mine –it's a miracle! We'll be contemplating on our stones side-by-side, seeing what they reveal. Where should we do our contemplation? A lake? A mountain?"

"I mind not – you can choose."

"Maybe we are on the cusp of a Golden Age for the Earth. Maybe the wheels have finally come around and connected, and this is it!"

"Yes, maybe. We shall have to see what the stones reveal. I have done my work with the stone for today. Each day expose yourself to the power of the stone for short periods only."

"I see. Just work with the stone for a few minutes."

"Yes. Now, about this 'feel-good' course." he said coyly. "Does it involve personal contact?"

"Are you talking about you and me? You and me being together?"

"I have never had any love in my life," he said pleadingly with his little boy eyes. "This is what is missing."

Georgina backed away a little. "To be honest, Zako, I am a little concerned about your psychosis. I am not trying to be heartless. I need to know more. What triggers it? What turns you into a psychopath?"

"Yes. What turns me into a psychopath?" Zakamonsky walked off, thinking about this. "My psychopathic-ness. What triggers it? Let me think. What is it that turns me into a raging psychopath?" He paced around the cinema thinking about it. Georgina looked a bit puzzled.

5

Fredrick observed Georgina and said to Hubert: "She is trying to make a decision here. It is sometimes difficult in deciding whether or not to have a relationship with a psychopath. It has to be said psychopaths do not have a particularly good reputation."

Hubert said, "No, they don't!"

"What would you advise?"

"I would advise against getting involved with a psychopath."

"But there are extraneous circumstances, like the future of the Earth. Perhaps the whole of the cosmos is dependent on this outcome. What would you say to that?"

Hubert scratched his head, trying to think his way through this conundrum. "It is a bit above my level, really, sir. I would rather not give an opinion on this, if that is all right with you."

6

Zakamonsky continued pacing the cinema and came up with an answer.

"Yes, every now and then I do become a psychopath; but what triggers it? I think it is betrayal. Yes, betrayal. That is what triggers it."

Georgina looked at him. "Betrayal?"

"Yes, it is betrayal that triggers it."

She got her hands ready in case he became psychotic again. "Betrayal: nothing else?"

"No, nothing else: just betrayal." He saw her hands at the ready. "It is not the words betrayal that make me psychotic, no, it is an actual betrayal."

She put her hands down.

"Actual betrayal and memories that trigger it. Like the betrayal of my father. Yes, the betrayal of my father." His face fell grimly as he thought about this. "Over and over, he betrayed me." His face became contorted with pain. "He betrayed me to the man who tried to steal my stone; betrayed me to him not once, but many times. That was not all he did." She put her hands on him.

"What else did he do?"

"He beat me. He used to beat me all night long."

Georgina shook her head. "That is bad," she said.

"Sometimes he used to beat me for weeks on end; sometimes months."

"He does not sound much of a Dad."

"No. That is not all he did. He tried to kill me."

"Oh."

"Several times, he tried to kill me."

"Oh dear, you did have a bad upbringing."

"Over one hundred and fifty times he tried to kill me. I spent all of my childhood trying not to get killed by him!"

"It is probably best not to think about your Dad. Come on, let us get you out of your psychosis." She sat him down on one of the seats and began applying her hands with more professionalism.

"It is not the killing; it is the betrayal," he said, moaning.

"Yes, well try not thinking about any of it."

"At every turn, he tried to thwart me." Zakamonsky broke down, shrieking: howling at the thought of it, his body convulsing. He was growing more and more psychotic – anger and fear taking hold. "Help me, help me!" Georgina realised he was going deeper into psychosis and applied her hands more vigorously. He did not respond. His breathing laboured; this was not a quick fix. He started whooping, his body sweating heavily. Georgina kept applying her hands. For several minutes, Georgina kept her hands going as Zakamonsky went through a deep trauma. Finally, he came out of it.

"Thank you," he said, depleted.

"That was a big one," she said, mopping his face.

"Yes, a big one."

"Are you better?"

Zakamonsky nodded weakly. "It must be destiny. You may be the only one in the universe that can help me out of my psychosis."

"Well, I am glad to help; me being the only one in the universe that can do this."

"I need some affection. Georgina, I need some affection. I have never had any affection in my whole life. For four and a half thousand years, I have not had one bit of affection. I am desperate for it." He looked at her with his little-boy eyes, lost; helpless.

Georgina was a little overcome by the helplessness of Zakamonsky. "What sort of affection were you looking for?"

"What sort of affection have you got?"

"There are different levels of affection."

"Are there? What is the top level?"

"The idea is, you start at the bottom level and work your way up."

“What is the bottom level?”

“Talking. That is the first level, and also the top level.”

“What would we talk about?”

“Our hopes, our fears. Our problems. Maybe our secrets.”

“I have never spoken to anyone about any of these things.”

“You know something, Zako, nor have I.”

“Do you want to talk about these things?”

“Yes, I do. I long to talk about these things, but never found anyone to do it with.”

“I feel the same way,” Zakamonsky said. “I long to talk to someone; have longed for centuries to talk to someone, but can I trust you? If I tell you things, can I trust you?”

“Yes, you can; you can trust me. You can tell me everything that is troubling you. Only if we trust each other can we talk about these things. Come on, let us dance.”

She led him led him to the back of the cinema where there was space and embraced him in an old-fashioned dance. “Let us dance and talk,” she said.

Zakamonsky sighed and sunk into her embrace as they danced. He melted into a gentle love he had never felt before. “I feel a huge weight coming of my shoulders,” he said. “This is so beautiful, Gina. I cannot tell you how beautiful this is. Love for the first time in my life! Thousands of years of pain are lifting.” Zakamonsky slowly spun her around, soaking up every ounce of this gorgeous cocoon of love.

Georgina was feeling it, too, and it was a surprise. "I never expected any of this, yet it feels right. It feels right to be with you."

Zakamonsky gasped in ecstasy. "Does it? Does it really feel right? Does that mean you will join me on my last five hundred years of life?"

"Join you on your last five hundred years of life?"

"You know it is in my gift to grant you five hundred years of life. I guess I have waited four and a half thousand years to connect with you. You, being the only one that understands the Earth stone. A four and a half thousand year wait, and you come with the ability to cure me of my psychosis; you come with the ability of love. Four and a half thousand years! Amazing!!"

"It is amazing! Four and a half thousand years, but why now?"

"I imagine it is because the Earth is nearing the end for humans in its present form. This is the last chance for humans and for my people to rehabilitate themselves on Earth. It has been left until the last moment."

"This is big; bigger than I ever thought possible. Are we to bring in the Golden Age?"

"I imagine this is what will happen. Will you join me on the last five hundred years of my life?"

In a raging fit of impetuousness, Georgina said, "Yes, I shall join you on your last five hundred years of life. We will go on a five hundred-year adventure together. We will be in love. We will talk. We will consult our stones. We will solve all the problems of the Earth. We shall rehabilitate your people. And we will have our own adventure of love as well."

"That sounds wonderful beyond my wildest dreams," Zakamonsky said, dissolving into a huge wave of love. "The final five hundred years to be lived out in love and bliss, spending it with a beautiful woman. My mission fulfilled; your mission fulfilled. The divinity of the universe can be perfect."

"You are a deep and expansive man, Mr Zakamonsky. It surprises me. It is also amazing to discover I am starting to feel very warm towards you. I feel a surprising empathy for everything you have gone through."

"That is so lovely to hear," Zakamonsky said, dancing much closer. "In a thousand years, they could be looking back and seeing the story between us and say it was the greatest love story of all time. Zakamonsky was the man who waited four and a half thousand years for his Goddess; the only one that could save him from his psychosis. Two people that saved the Earth, and brought in the Golden Age."

Georgina said, "I never expected anything quite as big as this – a five hundred-year love story; bringing in the Golden Age; being in love; talking…being close – sharing each other's secrets. It has everything! I am in!"

They danced; danced around the cinema whispering to each other; whispering their secrets; whispering their fears; whispering their innermost thoughts. They danced and danced, getting to know each other and becoming closer. They danced whispering, becoming stronger together. They danced around the cinema; danced several times past Squires. Finally, as the happy couple approached one more time, Squires took the opportunity to collar them.

"Ahum," Squires said. "Sorry to bother you at this happy moment, Mr Zakamonsky, but do you think there is a possibility of getting my body back to normal?"

Zakamonsky detached himself from Georgina. "Yes, Squires, of course. As soon as my scientists finish up with the Earth stone I will get them working on a formula to get you back to normal bodily situation."

5

Squires was elated. "Thank you very much, Mr Zakamonsky, very decent of you. Can I ask just one more thing?"

"Yes Squires, what is it"

"Are you and Miss Georgina going to rule the Earth?"

Zakamonsky said, "Yes, think so. That is the plan. Depends on the stones, of course." Georgina nodded. "Yes, me and Zako are going to rule the Earth. I am sure that is what the stones will say."

"Am I coming along?"

"Of course you are coming along," Georgina snapped. "You and Charlotte will be coming along!"

"Thank you very much. Can I ask if there will be any banks in this new set up of yours?"

"We have not decided yet, have we Zako?"

Zakamonsky said, "No, it depends a bit on the stones. What is on your mind, Squires?"

"I would not mind robbing some banks, just to tide me over. I shall be at your service, of course."

"For you, I shall create some banks so you can rob them. We can do that can't we?" Zakamonsky said, winking at Georgina. Georgina nodded and winked back.

"Very decent of you, Mr Zakamonsky. I had my doubts at first but can see now you are a really good bloke: an ace fella! Thank you."

"Not at all, Squires."

Charlotte looked bitter-sweetly at Zakamonsky and Georgina. "You two love birds. I am out in the cold now. I will not get a look in."

"There is Mr Squires," Georgina said.

"Squires?"

Georgina said, "Yes, why don't you two get together?"

Zakamonsky asked, "Are you up for that, Mr Squires? Having Charlotte as your partner?"

"Cor, yeah," Squires put his fingers around Charlotte's waist. "Hello, darlin'," he said.

"Get your dirty fingers off me, Squires."

Georgina looked around the room. "Come on, Sharls; there is nobody else. Mr Zakamonsky has agreed to give each of us an extra five hundred years of life so we can see in the Golden Age!"

"Isn't that great. Don't I get a say in any of this? What about my ideas? Aren't my ideas to be considered in this new and perfect world of yours?"

Georgina looked at Zakamonsky. "Can we consider Sharls's ideas?"

Zakamonsky said, "Yes, of course. What are your ideas?"

Charlotte had to think rapidly. "I am a human rights activist. I have many ideas. We could start with gay rights, LGBT rights, transgender rights…"

Zakamonsky scratched his chin. "Does Mr Squires agree with those ideas?"

Squires's fingers lingered by her waist, itching.

"I think you and Squires should submit your ideas as one unit."

"Me and Squires as one unit…isn't that great?"

"Come on, Sharls. We have always been together. We will have five hundred years of ruling the Earth. When you understand the stone and become a Goddess, you can join in."

After a bit of grumbling, Charlotte said: "Fine, OK, I am in."

Zakamonsky smiled. "Great I think we should celebrate. We should raise a toast." He walked over to a concealed drinks cabinet and poured four glasses of Champagne. He handed out each of the fluted glasses, and raised his own glass. "Let's do as they say in England, 'Bottoms Up'!"

Georgina raised the bottom of her glass. "Bottoms Up to Mr Zakamonsky," she said, and raised it for a second time, "and bottoms up to Mr

Zakamonsky for initiating this five hundred-year adventure for us; and bottoms up to Mr Zakamonsky for bestowing an extra five hundred years of life on us."

Clutching the glass with his fingers, Squires said: "Bottoms up mate! Thank you very much." He said to Charlotte, "Come on darlin', bottoms up to Mr Zakamonsky."

"Yes – bottoms up Mr Zakamonsky." Charlotte said.

"Let us all dance," Zakamonsky said.

Zakamonsky led Georgina off, dancing. "Look at them," Zakamonsky whispered. "Starting out. Trying to work it out."

"Come on darlin'," Squires said. "we are meant to be dancing; Mr Zakamonsky has said so."

"We will dance when I say so," Charlotte said. "We shall have terms of engagement. You must stick to my terms or I shall use my influence to cancel your re-materialisation."

"I see, my little chicken: a bit feisty. I want you to come out on my bank raids. You will be my moll. What you don't realise is that I have cards up my sleeve too. You need me to approve your plans before giving them to Mr Zakamonsky, hah, hah."

That was not the only card Squires had up his sleeve. He was thinking about his main asset: his dematerialised dematerialising gun. He could dematerialise her, bit by bit.

"Look at them two, so sweet!"

"They are working it out."

"We worked it out, didn't we?"

"Yes we did," Georgina purred like some contented cat. "It worked out better than I could have ever imagined. You getting my stone back; us coming together; going on a five hundred-year adventure; ruling the Earth together; consulting our stones; issuing decrees. I could not have imagined anything better."

Zakamonsky spun her around. "What are we going to do tomorrow? On day one?"

"We shall sit down and consult our stones and see what they tell us to do for day two."

"Anything else?"

"Five minutes of affection."

"Five minutes? Is that all I get?"

"It is open to negotiation. Life is a negotiation. Let us enjoy this evening."

They danced, folding into a sweet pool of love. Around they danced, Georgina getting a little drunk. "This is wonderful," she said.

"Yes, it is!" Zakamonsky emitted a sweet sigh of his own. "Look at Squires and your cousin. Even they are getting it together."

Squires and Charlotte did seem to be getting on, and were dancing, although Charlotte did have a sly look about her.

Georgina said, "It is perfect. The family together. Squires and Charlotte will have their own adventures. The First Family of Earth embarking on our five hundred-year reign. It is going to be so much fun."

"A strange family, it has to be said: a bank robber, a human rights activist and us."

"The universe has dealt us a strange hand, but it is perfect."

"Yes." Zakamonsky sank into Georgina, dancing in small circles, luxuriating in the way everything had worked out. For the first time in his life he felt free: free to express himself; free to tell his secrets; free to express his fears – which he did. He had never been happier.

All of a sudden, there was a great thumping on the wall. The door began shaking. Everyone stopped dancing, mystified. It was like there were builders outside with bulldozers in the process of knocking the building down.

It was not builders; it was something else.

CHAPTER NINE

1

"NO!!"

In Arizona, George and Figgis were about to be turned into pigeons. The aliens were about to break out from their concrete prison.

"No, we are not going to become pigeons! We are going to be proud human beings and do the right thing. Cancel the pigeon protocol immediately!"

Figgis, stunned by George's sudden authority, cancelled the pigeon order, but the sound of drilling above them was intensifying. The aliens were near to breaking through. "What are we going to do, sir?" Figgis asked, timidly.

"We are going to make a run for it. Can those gorillas run? Run faster than the robots outside?

"I don't know. They have bigger legs, so they probably could."

"That is what we will do. We will make a run for it. Can those gorillas carry us?"

"Well, yes. It is hard to explain, but yes, they can carry us."

"Order them to carry us now, Figgis! Make a dash for the aeroplane and take off as fast as you can!"

And that is what happened. They sped through the fortress, out of the door into the desert, and made a mad dash for the plane. The two million robots were taken by surprise, but were soon alerted. Only two caught up and they clung on to the little jet as it was taking off. Figgis had to flip the aircraft upside down several times and wriggle sharply to get them off. They had escaped. They had the white stone.

En-route, they got themselves re-materialised as they headed for California.

2

They landed at Santa Monica airfield, took a hire truck to the experimental cinema, and were now on the other side of the door into the cinema.

"Figgis, tell the gorillas to bash the door down!"

"Right-oh, sir." Figgis said, with a salute.

The gorillas gave the door a good crunching and kicked half the wall down, too. In amongst a pile of rubble they were in. Everyone in the cinema was startled.

George William caught site of the girls and Squires.

"A-ha! That is where you are. We have come to rescue you. Come away from the girls Zakamonsky!"

"No, Gramps"

"Figgis, get those gorillas to separate the girls from Zakamonsky!"

Figgis did as instructed. One gorilla held Zakamonsky at bay while the other pushed Georgina's party towards the rubble.

"George William, you don't understand," Zakamonsky shouted.

George ignored him, concentrating on Georgina. "Do you have the stone?"

Georgina, confused, produced her stone. It was still red, in the realm of Zakamonsky. George William transformed it with the powerful rays of the white stone.

"You are free," George said, triumphantly, as her stone returned to its beautiful but powerless golden glow.

"Ha-ha! You have lost, Zakamonsky," George William jeered. "Go back to your miserable, ugly planet. You will never have the Earth!"

An uncontrollable anger was building in Zakamonsky. "You will pay for this. I will bring you down, George William. I will destroy you." His body was becoming a crimson red.

"You are all bluster, Zakamonsky. Ciao! Arrivederci!"

The robots rapidly guided the girls and Squires out of the building. George William brushed his hands together, consummately proud of his commando operation.

"That is the way to do it, Figgis," he said.

"I see," Figgis nodded uncertainly.

Everyone bundled into the truck and within minutes they were at the Santa Monica airfield.

Minutes after, they were up in the air on the way back to Greece.

The girls were in shock.

George William came through from the cockpit to join them.

"Gramps we had it all sorted out. We were well on the road to sorting out a perfect solution for the future of the Earth with Mr Zakamonsky."

Like a protective grandfather, George William was stern: "You are better off without Zakamonsky."

"I was in love with him."

"Nonsense!"

"Mr Zakamonsky taught me how to be a queen to all people."

"Did he, now?"

"He taught me to be Queen of the Ganges and how to be like Aphrodite.

"Rascal! Trying to get some hanky-panky, no doubt."

"It is not like that. Mr Zakamonsky is a very deep person. He has got his faults; many very bad faults, actually. Deep down he is willing to learn and put them right. Underneath he is a very spiritual person. He taught me to become Zorya. We sailed down the Volga River and millions turned out for our dawn ceremonies; she is the Morning Star, who opens the gate for the sun to shine. They worshipped me as Zorya Uttrennyaya. It was the most beautiful experience of my life."

"Goddessy stuff, is it?"

"They are super-powers, Gramps. Super-powers for the good."

"Yes. Very useful. Well done."

"I want the stone."

"You have the stone; I have just saved your stone from the red realm."

Georgina got the Earth stone out of her velvet pouch and gazed at the beautiful, powerless gem. "Not this stone: the white stone."

George William slipped his hand into his cape and withdrew the white stone. It radiated a gorgeous, shimmering white: vibrant. Georgina was mesmerised. "Give it to me," she said.

"I think I should take care of it – if you don't mind," George William said, returning the gem back inside his cape.

Georgina glared at him; a frightening glare.

"Excuse me," he said, and retreated into the cockpit.

He said to Figgis: "She wants the white stone."

"Yes, I thought she might."

"Well she cannot have it."

"Why is that?"

"Because we should have it."

"Why?"

"Never mind why! Can you protect me from Georgina stealing the stone away from me?" He protectively covered the inside pocket with his hand.

Figgis shrugged, getting up from the pilot's seat, and locked the cockpit door. "I have one of the gorillas in the bathroom in case there is any trouble."

"That is very reassuring. You are a great individual, Figgis. Really a fine chap."

"Thank you, sir," Figgis said, and returned to the pilot's seat.

“So – have you made any progress in finding out who has been replacing the world leaders?’

Figgis smiled broadly. “Yes,” he said. “I have received a message.”

“Well?”

“Well, what?”

“What is the message?”

Figgis grinned and showed his boss a picture on his control panel. It was of two teeth: two elongated teeth.

“Is this it?”

“Yes,” Figgis said, grinning.

“Is it a rabbit? Is a rabbit replacing the world leaders?”

“Not a rabbit, no. It is Toothy Clive; he is the one.”

“Who is Toothy Clive?”

“He was in my class at robot school in Sheffield. That was thirty five years ago.”

“He was a classmate in your robot school?”

“Yes, that is right.”

“Does he have spots? Is he spotty?”

Figgis nodded. “Yes he does. He has spots and big teeth.”

“Isn’t that bloody marvellous? We have a spotty little nerd in charge of the world leaders. Can you get hold of him?”

“I can try.”

“Don’t try Figgis: do it! We do not want a spotty little nerd controlling world leaders. We need to be in control of the world leaders ourselves.”

CHAPTER TEN

1

Figgis headed as fast as he could to Athens International Airport, and onwards by chopper to the little island. Once everyone was despatched to their various quarters, Figgis made for his private den. In there, he set about locating Clive. It did not take long. He found a pair of teeth on the dark web, and entered into the protocol. It was Clive all right, and he came up on the screen.

"Hello Alo!"

"Aloysius, if you don't mind."

"Yeah, whatever. You have discovered it is me; I have been replacing world leaders." Clive grinned at him, boyishly, his two front teeth sticking out like rabbit chompers. With six large spots on his big, round, jovial face, he looked particularly nerdish and a bit demented.

Figgis grinned. "I have seen. How many world leaders have you done?"

"Enough."

"You got plans for them?"

"Not yet. Hoping you might have some ideas."

"I bet you want to use them for pranks."

"I do like a good prank." He paused a little before saying: "So do you!"

"It is true; I do like a good prank."

“Why don’t you join me? You could always think of a good prank. We could do pranks together with the world leaders.”

“You know, Clive, I have thought of some: I have one about the Prime Minister’s bottom, we could have it opening at awkward moments.”

Clive’s face lit up with excitement. “Yeah, that would be great. I knew you could think of good pranks.”

“I have some others.”

“Oh, Alo. Let us join together; you know we should.”

A little forlornly, Figgis said: “I am with George William now.”

“Does he like a good prank?”

“Sometimes. Not often.”

“He sounds an all-right bloke. Maybe I should join you.”

“He wants to rule the Earth.”

“Rule the Earth? That is a serious prank!”

“It is not a prank, Clive. He actually wants to rule the Earth. He has been thinking about this for the last two hundred years. I have been helping him for the last thirty years.”

“Oh.”

“He has an enemy called Mr Zakamonsky.”

“What does he do?”

“He is from another realm; he also wants to rule the Earth.”

“Does he like pranks?”

“I do not think so. I should be hooking into him in a few minutes. I can only do this once in a while. Would you like to see Mr Zakamonsky?”

"Yes please. Let us see Mr Zakamonsky; he might be fun."

"All right, I will rig it up and rig you in. It will take a few minutes."

2

Zakamonsky sat upstairs in the military wing of his imperial palace; behind his big formal desk. His face was ashen, quietly seething with intense anger. He had become psychotic. Without Georgina to cure him, it was getting deeper and more acute: free-falling into hidden depths. He was not pining to Georgina for help: the opposite. There was no way back. This was betrayal on a magnitude he had never before experienced. Georgina had summoned George William to rescue her, and not before she had performed a humiliation on him of such enormity that it was hard for him to comprehend; led him to the height of vulnerability and then struck. A seductress of immense callousness: betrayal on an unimagined scale! There was only one thing for it: revenge. He knew what he had do. He must eradicate the entire human population, leaving just Georgina and George William as the only humans left alive on Earth. Georgina and George William against him and the vast army of his empire. He would take his time thinking what to do with these two people. This gave him some comfort. They were now his deepest enemies. He ordered General Lout into the room.

Lout stood rigidly in front of Zakamonsky's desk.

"Lout, you are the most thuggish of all my generals, but a superb organiser – the best organiser I have ever had."

Lout stood to attention.

"I have a job for you to perform, but first I need to know one thing: would you betray me?"

"No, Supreme Commander. I perform best when serving a master; being second-in-command in a long chain of underlings. That is how I perform best, so it would be futile for me to betray you."

"Good. Perhaps you will be my right-hand man.

"Tell me your first name, Lout."

"Him, Supreme Commander."

"Him?"

"Him, yes; to reflect my masculinity. I train every day. I aspire to be the hardest man of all time. I am harsh with the troops. I do not tolerate disobedience."

Zakamonsky smiled a little. "Him…who must be obeyed?"

Lout nodded curtly. "Him: a name I adopted to keep me on track to look more masculine. I work out every day to look more masculine. I am looking more masculine daily: masculine in mind body and spirit; that is my aim."

"Him-Lout, I am going to promote you to second-in-command," Zakamonsky said. "I have a job for you. Eradicate the entire human population from Earth."

Him-Lout smiled briefly. “For the purity of your race? Yes, Supreme Commander, I understand.”

Zakamonsky looked puzzled. “I want the entire human race eradicated, apart from two people: Georgina Tipton, and George William. Leave Georgina Tipton and George William as the only human beings alive. Is this something you can take care of?”

Him-Lout nodded rigidly. “Yes, Supreme Commander. This is something I can undertake with efficiency.”

“You are not from here, Lout. When did you arrive?”

“Nineteen-forty-five, Supreme Commander. I have been here seventy-five years.”

Him-Lout stood erect the other side of the desk, a figure from the very bottom of the slug order; yet through sheer force of will, his face and parts of legs burst through his slug-like features, his stony face like granite.

Zakamonsky looked at Lout, darkly. “Despite you being from the lowest depths, you have strong will and shall help me in my hour of need. You are a despicable character, capable of using extreme force to achieve an objective. You are completely the right person for this situation. I need retribution. Come with me to the great laboratory hall.”

On the way down, Zakamonsky looked at Him-Lout and repeated: “You will not betray me?”

“No, Supreme Commander; I have said I perform best as second-in-command.”

They reached the great laboratory hall.

At this point, Figgis's transmission came on line. "We are in, Clive! Let us see what Mr Zakamonsky is doing."

3

Lout and Zakamonsky entered the great laboratory hall. Five thousand scientists were working diligently at their lab stations.

Zakamonsky nodded grimly at Lout. "All these scientists are at your disposal. I suggest their work be diverted to developing an irreversibly lethal virus in a very short space of time."

"Understood, Supreme Commander." Him-Lout said with a blunt nod.

"Remember, I want George William and Georgina left alive. They should be the only humans left alive on Earth; I have a special punishment for those two."

"All humans to be annihilated apart from George William and Georgina Tipton," Lout said, nodding stiffly.

"Georgina Tipton betrayed me and I have a very special punishment for her. First, I need to wipe out humanity and see how she feels about that. I shall leave now, to contemplate my punishments for her and George William. My soul needs to be soothed with retribution."

"Leave all this to me, Supreme Commander," Him-Lout said.

Zakamonsky left the hall and Him-Lout ordered ten thousand of his soldiers into the hall. They came streaming in, marching in their jackboots, and lined up and sealed off the laboratory hall.

Lout, flanked by ten soldiers, headed down the hall to have a conversation with the Chief Scientist, who was sitting on his little throne.

"I am in charge now," Him-Lout said, cracking his whip at the Chief Scientist. "Turn this entire hall over to creating a virus one hundred per cent lethal to humans."

The Chief Scientist's face dropped, crestfallen, his imminent redemption disintegrating before his eyes.

"I want this done with extreme speed. Within one month, the entire human population should be dead. Dead, infected with your virus. That is what is required of you. I have ten thousand soldiers with whips to encourage the progress. You will obey me completely." He signalled to his ten-thousand soldiers, who all cracked their whips and stamped their boots. The sound was eerie and overwhelming.

Figgis's transmission faded out. Both Figgis and Clive were gob-smacked.

"I was not expecting something quite as bad as this," Figgis declared.

Clive shook his head. "You are right, I don't think Mr Zakamonsky is into pranks. Those two blokes want to wipe out all humans…that includes us. What are we going to do, Alo?"

"We could become pigeons."

"Pigeons?"

“Yes, I have discovered how to become a pigeon. Just before the virus hits, we could become pigeons.”

“Thanks, Alo, I’ll join you in pigeon world; but what about our pranks?”

“We can keep working on the pranks until the virus hits. I am glad you got in touch.”

“So am I. I want to be with you, Alo.”

“Me too. Tell me Clive – I have been out of touch for the last thirty years – you and me concentrated on robots, but the world is now being run by computers: banks, government services, shopping, everything is being run by computers. Who is behind this?”

“That would be Mikey’s lot from the other class: the class downstairs – the ‘lower class’.”

“The ‘lower class’?” Figgis was riled.

“Yes, Mikey’s mob went on to open programming schools, and expanded all across the world. The world’s computers systems are being programmed by students from Mikey’s schools.”

Figgis said grimly: “All being done by Mikey’s mob from the ‘lower class’.”

“What are you thinking, Alo?”

“We cannot let Mikey’s mob get away with this. Can we hack into them?”

“Course we can; we are from the top class.”

“Let us do it, Clive. We will take over the world’s computer systems from Mikey’s lot. I will think up pranks we can do all day long!”

“Yeah, Alo, I am with you on this. I will pack my bags and come to Greece.”

"It will be so much fun. The world will be hilarious with us running it."

"I am glad we have re-connected. There is this virus though."

"Oh yes."

Both their faces fell.

"The virus and Mr Zakamonsky's plan to get rid of humans."

"Yes," Figgis said after a bit. "Yes, I had better tell George William about this right away."

Clive said. "Yes, let me know what happens."

4

Figgis found George William out on the north terrace, relaxing into a glass of whiskey.

"Figgis, ole boy! Any luck with locating the toothy wonder?"

"Yeah, but I have something else to tell you. Something more serious."

"What is that?"

"Mr Zakamonsky is planning to wipe out the human race."

"Is he?" George William put his whiskey down. "How do you know that?"

Figgis replayed the transmission from Zakamonsky's laboratory hall - Zakamonsky authorising Him-Lout to use the five thousand scientists to develop a lethal virus to eradicate the human population; annihilate the whole human population apart from Georgina Tipton and George William. George William's face dropped. He watched it all with growing horror, and his face turned white.

"Oh Lord! What are we going to do?"

"He seems to want to single you and Georgina out for some grim punishment," Figgis said.

"This is an unmitigated disaster."

"Looking back birdland would not have been a bad choice, would it?"

"We cannot let Zakamonsky wipe out humans with his virus. What can we do?"

"I don't know. You could have a word with him, tell him to stop."

"Have a word? A word! He would half strangle me before I got anywhere near him."

Figgis shrugged.

George William took to marching up and down the terrace, thinking. "I know what we should do," he said finally.

"What is that?"

"We will get Georgina to have a word with him."

"Miss Georgina? He hates her too."

"Figgis, what you need to understand is that this is a war-like situation. In a war-like state of affairs, you have to face up to circumstances and deal with them. We should get Georgina to deal with them."

"That is a particularly unchivalrous thing for you to do, if you do not mind me saying so."

"Nonsense! She sees herself as a warrior: Georgina Warrior Princess. Let us see how she gets on."

“That is the most ungentlemanly thing I have ever heard.”

“Absolutely wrong. They are all liberated women now. We will send her into battle with the express mission of getting Zakamonsky to back down. This will test her metal. Summons the girls and set up a Privy Council meeting!”

5

Over on the south terrace, the mood was despondent. The dream had abruptly been torn apart and the sense of loss was palpable. They were trying to regroup and decide what to do next. Squires was lingering behind Charlotte with his fingers itching, wondering if it was still on, or not.

Georgina was staring at her beautiful but powerless stone. “We need to get the white stone out of the hands of Gramps,” she decreed.

Charlotte asked, “Why?”

“We need to get my stone back on full power in the Earth realm.”

“I thought we had been through this: we would get stuck in other realms before we get to the Earth realm; it is far too dangerous; we cannot do it!”

“That is exactly why we need the white stone. As soon as we enter the wrong realm, we will use the white stone to get us back. We will only be in a wrong realm for a few seconds. Squires could hold the white stone in his fingers and shine it at the Earth stone as soon as we enter a wrong realm."

"What if he drops it? He has no hands, only fingers."

"I will not drop it, darlin'," he said to Charlotte. "I will hold firm."

"He might become incapacitated; we might all become incapacitated," Charlotte said, and continued arguing through a long list of possible scenarios that could go wrong. "It is far too risky," she kept saying.

She was cut short by the arrival of Figgis.

Georgina looked Figgis up and down. "Have you come up with a solution for getting the Earth stone back on full power?" she asked.

"No, Miss Georgina. I have come about a very serious matter: Mr George William is convening a Privy Council meeting in half-an-hour and wants you to attend."

"What is the topic of this meeting?" Georgina probed.

"I think it best Mr George William tell you himself."

"Come on, Mr Figgis, spit it out!"

"All right," Figgis said shyly, "Mr Zakamonsky has turned mental. He is going to wipe out the human race."

"Oh dear! Zako's turned psychotic and it is much worse than I imagined. All because Gramps came storming in like the Fifth Cavalry. How did you find this out, Mr Figgis?"

Figgis reluctantly replayed his transmission, which Georgina, Charlotte and Squires watched. Georgina remained poker faced.

"What does Gramps intend to do about this situation?" she asked.

"I think I'd better let George William tell you that himself."

Figgis left, and a few minutes later, Georgina's party made their way over to George William's side of the house.

6

George William had - rather pompously - set up a table adorned with various regalia for his Privy Council meeting. He was seated at the head of the table in a high-backed chair, and on his head rested a crown; not a real crown, but one temporarily fashioned out of tin: silly-looking, really. Georgina and Charlotte sat on opposite sides of the table. Squires's fingers lingered behind Georgina and awaited orders from her.

When everyone settled, George William brought his gavel down on the table. "I have brought you here today because a matter of the uttermost seriousness has been brought to my attention."

Georgina said, "You talking about Mr Zakamonsky's plan to infect almost the entire human population with his virus."

"Ah, you have heard."

"Yes, he wants to kill off the human population and just leave you and me."

"We cannot let this happen," George William bleated. "We cannot let the whole of humanity die."

"What is the plan? What are you planning to do about it?"

"I was hoping you could talk with him and reason with him."

"Mr George William," Georgina said formally, "Mr Zakamonsky has gone psychotic; deeply psychotic. There is no way anyone can reason or talk to him at the present time. Maybe not for two months. He is too far gone. In two months, Mr Lout could have released the virus and killed the human population."

"There must be something we can do."

"Give me the white stone," Georgina demanded.

George William took the shining white stone out from his cape. He looked at it, and put it back. "I think it best I keep it for safe-keeping," he said.

Georgina clicked her fingers at Squires.

Squires shot around the table and put his fingers around George William's neck. "Give her the bloody stone," he said.

"Sit down, Squires, there's a good chap."

Squires tightened his grip. George squealed.

"Loosen up, Squires," Georgina ordered. "Let him give it to me in his own way!"

Squires loosened, and George William regained some composure. He released the white stone from the inside pocket of his cape. "Yes, of course you should have it. Take good care of it." He gave the stone to Squires.

Squires brought the white stone to Georgina, and she placed it in a second velvet purse. "Right, I shall take my party to California and try and sort out the horrendous mess you have put us all in: the horrendous mess you have created for all human beings."

George William looked pitifully repentant. "I am sorry, truly sorry. What can I do to help?"

"You can get Mr Figgis to fly us to California."

Figgis was not present at the table. He was a few yards away behind some bushes, looking at his screen and chatting to new-found pal Clive.

"Figgis…Figgis!" George William yelled.

Figgis said to Clive: "Forget coming to Greece, Clive; we will meet up in California."

"Yeah, alright Alo!"

An hour later Figgis, the girls and Squires left for California.

7

"Well," Fredrick said. "We are still no clearer in deducing who will prevail in taking over the Earth."

"No sir. It is a murky picture."

"There is still no front-runner that could determine the future of the human race."

"I should point out, sir, that very soon there may not be a human race."

"You are right," Fredrick said, sombrely. "That Him-Lout is definitely a spanner in the works. A nasty determined individual with horrible form. Done terrible things in the past. This is a very serious business; it is becoming a brutal affair. A very real possibility exists that the human race could be wiped out by Him-Lout."

Fredrick and Hubert went silent as they came to terms with the awesome seriousness of the situation. It was like they were in a wake.

After a while Fredrick said,

"Assuming Him-Lout does not succeed, and is somehow overcome, and using your instinct, which of the three parties do you feel may prevail? At this halfway stage, which of the three do you feel is most likely to succeed?"

"Well, sir, it could be four contenders."

"Do you mean Mr Figgis?"

"Yes."

"You could be right. Figgis and his spotty chum seem to have formed a fourth party. In some ways, they are the most capable at taking over the Earth. The human part of the Earth at any rate."

"I need to point out again: there may not be a human part of the Earth!"

"Hmmm … you are right, but I still think we should get in with Figgis and his spotty chum; I believe they could be useful."

"I know you have some plan up your sleeve. Would you mind telling me what it is?"

"It is not the right time to reveal my hand, Hubert. What I can say about the situation is this: with Mr Zakamonsky being psychotic and General

Lout running riot, I see a battle royal on the horizon. I can say with some certainty that things are hotting up!"

CHAPTER ELEVEN

1

Zakamonsky, grimly deepening in his psychosis, took up residence in a villa dug high into the Hollywood Hills. An isolated northern part of the Hollywood Hills; it was at the peak of a lonely canyon in the Santa Monica mountains. The smell of sagebrush lingered from the hot arid terrain of the day, but by night it was cold and a lone mountain lion roamed around the canyon. Him-Lout was in residence in the villa at the top of the canyon too. Hour by hour Zakamonsky's psychosis deepened, and he went to sleep dreaming of revenge.

At first light Zakamonsky got up.

The villa was set back 200 feet away from the cliff face. Here at the edge was a viewing platform. From it he gazed down at the vast metropolitan conurbation of Greater Los Angeles. An expansive view with seemingly endless lines of parallel dead-straight thoroughfares. Rows and rows of them spread out on the massive flat plain below him. Houses and businesses in neat lines that stretched many miles into the distance. Somewhere in the middle, perhaps twenty miles away, a small collection of stick-like objects poked up in a haze.

Downtown Los Angeles. He contemplated the gigantic plain beneath him. A plain in which millions of people lived and worked.

Him-Lout joined him on the viewing platform.

Zakamonsky said to him, "I want every human removed from here. Every human apart from Georgina Tipton and George William,"

Him-Lout nodded and surveyed the scene with his binoculars, and they came to rest on the Los Angeles Memorial Coliseum eighteen miles away. L.A.'s premier stadium and sporting venue. With a compacity of around eighty thousand it had hosted two Olympic Games, and was due to host a third. Commissioned in 1921 it was a memorial to veterans of the first world war; and Him-Lout smiled a little at the poetic irony of this.

"Supreme Commander I have a plan to fill the stadium to capacity and experiment with drones fitted with aerosols," Him-Lout said. "I estimate fifty drones to be sufficient to spray everyone throughout the stadium with the new virus. I wish to test the effectiveness of this and adjust my strategy accordingly."

Zakamonsky looked away. "I do not want to know how you are going to do it. I simply need it done. Now go, leave me. I wish to contemplate n silence."

After Him-Lout had gone Zakamonsky regained his contemplations and continued looking at the vast plain spread out below him. Imagining it with everyone gone. All humans removed. He would have Georgina driven around the lifeless city by the robots and forced to view mile after mile of empty buildings. Everyone last one of them empty of humans. A city without humans. Nothing, all gone. All human life gone. Nobody there. A city void of humans that was all down to her, her betrayal. He would get the robots to open all the doors and windows of houses and businesses in a thirty mile radius and drive her around them. Now and then they would stop and inspect, and the robots would say to her. "Nobody in here. Everyone gone. Everyone gone from this street. Gone because of your betrayal," and then move on to the next few blocks.

After a few hours of this he would have her taken to the studios. The studios he had captured. All of the studios that would have been hers. Show her what could have been. Let her contemplate that. All that could have been. So many things she was to be given. So many things to have been shared. Thrown away because of her betrayal. He felt a moment of extreme pain and sadness, sorrow at what could have been, and then blocked it out. He was used to deep hurt, blocking it out and becoming a rock. A rock that would carry on with the job. The job at hand now was to give retribution for being tricked. It would not end with Los Angeles. After she had seen the studios, and taken that in, the robots would take her on a world tour. Show her country after country.

The entire world. Every country devoid of humans. Humanity ended because of her betrayal. The end of the human race, all down to her. Her the only female left on the entire planet. How deliciously lonely she would be. Lonely just like him. Only two humans left alive on earth. Her and George William, but George William would be unreachable, locked up in a far-away impenetrable prison. His thoughts moved on to the earth without humans.

Now an earth without humans he could go on to populate it with his own people. Concentrate on the core mission of his existence. Rehabilitating his own people. The mission he had been entrusted with and been anointed to do. His mission would become easier. A planet empty of humans. No need for invasion. No silly ideas of co-operating with humans. Creating a golden age for the earth with Georgina, a doomed idea of the past. He would populate it with his people, and bring in a new beginning for the earth. Rehabilitate his own people and return them to the beautiful intelligent beings they were intended to be. Rehabilitate his fallen race. That would be the golden age for earth,

Then he thought about the punishment for George William. Maybe incarceration would be enough. That would teach him his folly. After all it was two hundred since his first incarceration where he thought up the ridiculous idea of a perfect world empire for humans. Now he could see that there were not any humans to have a perfect world empire for. After he could see that idea was irrevocably dead, he would either give up in desperation or join him. Who knows, after a suitable interval of rehabilitation he may even take on George William as some kind of partner. Who could say?

Zakamonsky was already starting to feel better. In his demented state he was clear he was doing the right thing.

He summoned Him-Lout.

"Him-Lout," he said. "I am about to give you tools that will assist you in disposing of the world-wide human population."

2

Him-Lout stood impassively before him; waiting to hear more about these 'tools'. Unlike Zakamonsky, who appeared human and princely, Him-Lout was stuck at the very bottom of the slug order, with sludge. His face though was trying valiantly to burst out; hard as granite.

"I need to cover you up Him-Lout. I cannot afford to have anyone seeing you. I shall dress you with a full-length coat, a hat and a face-mask."

Him-Lout was affronted. "A face-mask, Supreme Commander?"

"Suspicion must not be aroused. Nobody should see someone as despicable as you."

"I will wear a face mask," Him-Lout agreed grimly.

Him-Lout was dressed.

Zakamonsky said "We shall leave for the desert."

Zakamonsky guided Him-Lout to a garage at the back. There were ten vehicles in the garage; nine specialised in irregular terrain, big wheeled paramilitary monsters, each designed for a different terrain: mud, water, mountain-face. Zakamonsky had them all. He didn't choose any of these. The one they got into was the tenth, a chunky Niro self-charging SUV. Him-Lot sat in the passenger seat while Zakamonsky drove down a dirt road at the back of the canyon.

Coming out of the canyon they were soon on the open highway in the 'high desert'. They were heading for the secret underground Mojave robot manufacturing base.

The desert was open and expansive. Dry, gritty sand, with a number of Joshua Trees. Forty five minutes later they reached the dry flat desert town of Palmdale; population 50,000. A few miles of single story houses, well-spaced, they passed a Sizzlers steak and buffet restaurant, which was closed. They turned onto 70th SE; and into open desert once more. Him-Lout sat silently in the passenger seat gazing out the flat featureless stretches of gritty desert sand punctuated only with the odd Joshua Tree.

"Where are we going?" Him-Lout asked.

"You'll see."

After a few minutes Zakamonsky turned right onto E Avenue I, Lancaster. Lancaster was the next town after Palmdale, but one could not see the town of Lancaster; it was miles away somewhere in the distant desert-scape. These roads and many like them where laid out long ago, in order these desert cities could expand outwards. Then onto 140th Street Lancaster, now far far away from Lancaster; and into the remoteness of the desert. Here the desert was even more feature-less. Miles of pale-coloured sand, coarse, hard sand, stretching as far as the eye could see. On the left side the desert was turning whiter and more arid – a bright dirty-white sand; and salty. Zakamonsky went off road. Simultaneously the SUV went into camouflage mode.

"We are coming into a restricted zone," Zakamonsky said.

No sooner had he said this than a huge bat-like aircraft steaked into view about five miles away. It came in low and appeared to land. A minute later a rocket jet flew in on the same trajectory.

"The top-secret testing site for the Earth's most advanced aircraft," Zakamonsky said.

"You own this base; this testing site for the Earth's most advanced aircraft is yours?"

"No, my robot manufacturing plant is underneath the aircraft testing site."

"What is the purpose for having a robot manufacturing plant beneath an aircraft testing site, Supreme Commander?"

"Mr Aloysius Figgis built the base underneath the air-force base twenty five years ago. He enjoys watching planes take off. Mr Figgis is like a child. He installed a periscope on one of the runways. He delights in looking at aircraft. Many of his bases are underneath air-force bases. Like a child he is."

"Mr Figgis owns this robot manufacturing plant?"

“No – I captured it from him.” Zakamonsky paused with the first glimmer of a smile since his psychosis began. “This base is all mine!”

They drove silently across the desert for a few miles as Him-Lout assimilated the fact that the Supreme Commander’s robot manufacturing base was beneath the world’s most advanced aircraft testing site.

Half mile to the left they were now parallel with a flat brilliant cream-white hard-impacted sea of salt – Rogers Dry Lake – which facilitated the multiple landing strips of the air-force base. The air was hot and very dry, a pungent acrid smell from the salt. The dry lifeless lake stretched for over eight miles. It was five miles wide. A few minutes later they arrived at the concealed entrance of Zakamonsky’s (formerly Figgis’s) underground robot manufacturing plant.

Inside the plant is was suddenly cool. They dropped down two levels. A robot greeted them and drove Zakamonsky’s SUV into a car park. Robots were everywhere busy doing jobs. Zakamonsky transferred into a golf-cart and drove Him-Lout to a metalled walkway which was fifty feet above the main manufacturing plant.

Looking down there were twelve parallel production lines, each about quarter of a mile long, each assembling body parts for new robots. All lines moving swiftly. Well organised lines of robots being manufactured for the days quota. Only two lines were producing soldier robots, others constructing humanoid robots for Zakamonsky’s pet projects. This rolling process was precise and quiet; eerily quiet. Him-Lout nodded silently with a little smile. At the end of the line the new robots stood up and were escorted by a chaperoning robot into a second hall. Here hundreds of robots installed the artificial intelligence elements of the robots make-up; and they did this with the precision of a surgeon. Then, riding the golf-cart, onto a third hall; an even larger hall. This quality tested the new robots; hundreds of private booths were in use as each new robot was extensively interrogated by monitoring robot; question and response interrogation to test the quality of the robots intelligence. Almost every robot had a unique intelligence programme and about ten percent failed the test and were discarded. Zakamonsky drove the cart onto the final hall; the gymnasium where the motor abilities of each robot was tested.

Zakamonsky got out of the cart. "I run a quality show here, Lout. Make sure it stays that way."

Him-Lout removed himself from the cart too, and stood rigidly to attention. "You should expect nothing less of me, Supreme Commander."

Zakamonsky moved off; and stopped abruptly, looking Him-Lout up and down, he said to him. "You are a ruthless despicable individual and I want to know one thing. Will you betray me?"

Him-Lout shook his vehemently. "Betrayal is something I will not do."

"Good. We shall move on to initiate you into the high command of this base."

They took a service elevator down a level into Zakamonsky's private communication room with Chief Robot Robert.

Zakamonsky sat down at the control board and pressed a few buttons. A screen lit up and the cheery face of Chief Robot Robert was on it.

"Greetings Lord Z. It is good to be in your presence once again."

Zakamonsky smiled. He liked Robert. "It is good to see you, too. I have new plans I am working on. I wish to change the command structure of this base."

"Change the command structure?" Robert asked cautiously.

"I need to take time off from the responsibilities of running this base in order to contemplate. I have been betrayed Robert, betrayed! I need time to soothe my soul."

Robert's concern was increasing. "You are resigning, Lord Z?"

"Not resigning, no. Soothing my soul. Taking time off to contemplate and consider my next move. Work out the next phase of my mission. General Lout will assume command while I take time-off."

Robert looked at Him-Lout disapprovingly. "Should we not devise some security checks before carrying out such huge structural change."

"General Lout is a competent General. The most competent General I have ever had."

"Betrayal Lord K. Betrayal is not uncommon at the top of leadership."

"General Lout has said he will not betray me. He has assured me several times he will not betray me."

"Possibly what General Lout says and what General Lout does are not the same thing."

"Robert," Zakamonsky snapped, "I have instilled a code of honour amongst my senior generals. A code to be truthful."

"Maybe when you are not there they could disobey your codes."

"My orders are always obeyed!" Zakamonsky roared.

"Once General Lout is installed into a command position he will be in a position to usurp you."

Zakamonsky thumped his fist up and down on the counter. "Nobody usurps me!" Zakamonsky thundered. "In my realm nobody would dare usurp me. Install General Lout into a command position now!"

"Are you certain about this, Lord Z?"

"Yes. I need to be relieved of my responsibilities so that I can soothe my soul."

Him-Lout stood rigid and devastatingly unemotional. Robert looked sternly in Him-Lout's eyes. "Raise your right hand, General Lout, and place it on the screen."

Lout put his hand on the screen. "Do you pledge allegiance to upholding the integrity of this base?" Robert asked, viewing Him-Lout with utmost suspicion.

"I do," Him-Lout said.

"Keep your hand on the screen while it is minutely scanned," Robert said.

Him-Lout kept his hand rigid while this process was carried out.

"Now place your head up against the screen, "Robert said.

Him-Lout placed his head against the screen while it was scanned. When it was fully scanned he released his head.

Robert stared at Him-Lout grimly. "General Lout you are now a commander of this base. I am compelled to carry out anything you order of me."

Him-Lout nodded curtly, not betraying any emotion.

Zakamonsky looked on, relieved. "Thank you Robert," he said, "we shall re-unite soon. After I have soothed my soul for the betrayal I have suffered. I crave the freedom to soothe my soul."

Zakamonsky left the base with Him-Lout and drove to the Hollywood Hills.

Back on his canyon Zakamonsky looked at Him-Lout. "I shall now be free to soothe my soul. I shall enter into a period of deep contemplation secure in the knowledge you will carry out my orders. I shall be absent now for several weeks."

"Yes Supreme Commander," Him-Lout said.

Zakamonsky retired into a contemplation temple he had built at the bottom of the garden.

3

Him-Lout had no intention of following Zakamonsky's orders; he had plans of his own. He could not believe his luck. The possibilities the Mojave manufacturing plant offered were vast. Obviously production would be increased and expanded, with worldwide manufacturing plants added, but this was not what he was thinking about. He walked out of the villa to the edge of the cliff and onto the viewing platform. He raised his binoculars and adjusted the focus on the Los Angeles Memorial Coliseum. His first mission was to get that stadium filled and exterminate the crowd. The first part of this mission was to return to the science lab and expediate production of the lethal virus. And to recruit a colleague.

Meanwhile Figgis and Georgina's party had landed in Los Angeles, and installed themselves at a beach-front hotel in the town of Santa Monica; roughly twenty five miles from Zakamonsky's lair in the Santa Monica mountains.

Also, at about the same time, Clive arrived in Los Angeles. After thirty years Figgis and Clive were re-uniting on the mezzanine level of the Santa Monica beach-front hotel, while waiting for the girls to freshen up.

Hello, I'm the author...

Yes, it is hotting up; and I hope you will come back to see what happens in the final part of Global Takeover. Expect the unexpected, I think you will be pleasantly surprised.

The addition of Him-Lout is very recent and potentially very risky too. Looking back it seems madness for a novice author like me to attempt such a complex mix of realities. He may come out altogether or turn into a purely fictional being. Let's see how it goes.

I know I am entering a lion's den by publishing and hope you'll treat me gently. I am a first time novelist and, foolishly, have not sought any professional help. Help with writing this book that is, but probably need help in the head too! I am battering down for a public mauling for being an incompetent literary ignoramus, but hope instead your feedback will escort me firmly but compassionately into making this a great fantasy saga, which I am thinking it could be. That is the hope.

To the thorny issue of why I am publishing the third part before the first: yes. After I wrote the first book (set in the 1800's) something held me back from attempting to publish. I wrote the second book and the same happened. It was turning into a never-ending monster. I know what it was now. The series was progressively becoming an ever-deeper fantasy; the true extent of which, particularly concerning Mr Zakamonsky. He's a strange chap Zakamonsky isn't he? A bit of an enigma too. A severely damage fellar I would say, but (I think) redeemable. He seems to reveal new aspects of himself (to me) as we go along. Anyway, I feel I now know enough about the variety of strange world's most of the characters inhabit to feel on firmer ground to plough ahead with a public appearance. Also, after three and a half years, I am getting a little desperate to get something out there.

Clive too recently popped up out of nowhere and I am glad he did. Figgis and Clive together are proving to be amazingly funny. I have written two further chapters since this was published, and Clive and Figgis are very amusing, particularly the way the deal with Him-Lout, which does seem to make the reality of him less likely to zone you out. Maybe this is what Dystopian Comedy is. I am considering pitching for a film series featuring Clive and Figgis – not with Him-Lout I should add.

Although most of Global Takeover has been spontaneous the ending has been set for quite some while. I think you will like it and wager you will never guess it even though the clues are there!

About me

I've messed about in films. Currently I'm a highly inexperienced novice author writing the third part of the Tipton Saga. I live on the south coast of England, close to the beach, in the county of Sussex. I plan to do some events. If you are in Sussex, or visiting Sussex, come along. At some point I am planning to resurrect the 'FeelGoodFilmClub'. This is a social event with buffet – showing great films and chat. With the current pandemic and yo-yo government I doubt that will happen before Spring 2022, but shall do other events before that. I have a website (www.dayfilm.com) It was hacked. I am starting to rebuild, but it is rather bare bones right now. You can get in touch through the website, and I would appreciate any comments. Thank you for reading and now for the previous two books, *the story so far.*

Philip Davidson

The Tipton Saga - the story so far

...

Book One
'The Long Wait'
(80,000 words approx.)
Long Synopsis

High above the Ohio River a 19th-Century trunk is delivered to Charlotte Tipton's house in present-day Pittsburgh. The Tipton family have lived in fear of this trunk ever since the original Charles Tipton locked it in a Philadelphia vault following his escape from England in 1850. The legend goes: 'The Devils from Danzig' will get them if they open it. There is a flashback to the origins of the Tipton family.

At midnight on 31st December, 1809 (New Year's Eve), George William performs a 'sacred duty' with a scullery maid called Nefeli. Late September 1810, twins are born. George and Charles, they are named, and they're immediately taken off to an orphanage near Tipton in England's industrial Black Country. Two weeks later, George William initiates a trust for these twins, and a week after that he is declared insane, and incarcerated for the rest of his life.

George and Charles grow up in the orphanage. One night in 1818, George Tipton wakes at 3am. His dormitory is bathed in the red-orange glow from the all-night furnaces. There is something magical about this light, and George finds he can communicate psychically with his mysterious father, who tells him he is unable to visit because he is locked up; young George assumes his father is in prison. They play games of ruling the world.

By daytime, George and Charles go to school. They are hated by the other orphans because of schooling provided by their strange anonymous trust. They have a science teacher called Horatio Figgis, who introduces the twins to the world's first photographic camera, and their music teacher takes them to a first performance of Beethoven's Fifth Symphony. These two events set George on the road to make animated pictures with music. The first attempt is strictly against the rules of the Trust (after George William was incarcerated, a courtier modified the terms of the trust), and Charles spearheads an attempt to steal the plates before they are developed. He need not have bothered because the development process was a failure. George is exhilarated by the camera and harasses Figgis to perfect the developing process. Figgis breaks into a chemical works to obtain a missing chemical and accidentally sets the place alight, which results in a fireball that destroys the building. Mr H Figgis goes on the run and holes up in a fugitive colony near Liverpool. (Much later, George William orders a courtier to offer assistance to Figgis.)

George continues to make music-picture-stories and communicate with his father at night, although still not aware of his true identity. He is in communication with his Dad as he dies on 29th January, 1820. Strangely, King George III dies at the same time and the country goes into mourning.

As they grow up, Charles is the more successful brother, and becomes head lawyer to a major ironworks producing rail track to the burgeoning railway industry. At night, he organises union membership. Meanwhile, George becomes a clerk at the East India Company. At night, George makes music-picture-stories. Dozens are made, but he struggles to get a showing. One day, at the East India Company, he solicits a tea buyer to invest in his music-picture-stories and promptly gets the sack. He travels to Birmingham to beg his trustees for money but they refuse, saying Charles is more deserving. In a fit of jealousy, George tells the trustees Charles is organising union meetings, which is now legal, but considered distasteful. A week later, Charles is arrested, tried and jailed for sedition. George is horrified and confused, but accepts a small allowance from the trustees. He lives with guilt and fear of his brother. Years go by. George makes hundreds of music-picture-stories and goes mad with frustration as he cannot get a showing anywhere. In a desperate last throw, he reaches for the jackpot: his own personal theatre in the world's greatest exhibition of the 1800's – The Great Exhibition of 1851.

To enter the exhibition, George pitches to an Allocations Board, and shows a selection of his music-picture-stories. The Board are thoroughly impressed, and recommend his application. They requisition a theatre in south London for George to practise in. George is ecstatic and visits the site of the exhibition, which is in Hyde Park, London. The main building is a massive glass edifice called the Crystal Palace. It is three-quarters built, but being a Sunday the building is empty. George enters and realises it is not entirely empty; his estranged brother, who he has not seen for seventeen years, is there. Terrified, he climbs a wooden scaffold tower to attempt an escape through the roof. On the fiftieth tier, Charles pins him down and demands George hand over the theatre to him; to which George reluctantly agrees.

For several days George is forced to make animated pictures for a Charles's show. George is distressed he cannot stand up to Charles and goes to an East London gym to get boxing lessons from a tough cauliflower-eared trainer. In the midst of training, he remembers the magical red-orange light of his childhood, becomes a superman, and knocks out the trainer. Now empowered, he feels ready to take on his brother. That night, his mother (half-ghost, half-physical) visits and tells him the power is coming from an orange-red stone and presents him a white stone, should he ever get in trouble with the red-orange light.

The next day, Charles is having a dress rehearsal. George bides his time and watches the show. The show ends: George is about to strike, when a trumpet sounds and a royal messenger enters the theatre and invites George to Buckingham Palace. Everyone vanishes, including Charles. George finds Charles hiding underneath the stage, and discovers Charles has developed a pathological fear of royals. It is the result of years of being beaten by guards in the prison quarries for his so-called anti-royal sentiments. This in-turn is because of his trumped-up sedition charge which falsely stated he intended to harm and 'embarrass' the king on a visit to Wolverhampton. Now confused and deranged he fears the royals are out to get him. George takes pity on Charles and suggests they swap places at the audience with Prince Albert to prove his fears are unfounded. George instructs Charles on what to say about the show, and the original plan for the theatre is back on track.

In the morning, at the audience, Charles goes off script saying it will be a 'workers' theatre' and will be encouraging union membership. Prince Albert assumes it is a comedy and says he will look forward to watching it.

Going back to the theatre, George is flabbergasted and assumes Charles has become deranged again. However, Charles reveals he was trying to replicate conditions that led to his own arrest so George would go to prison and they would become equal. George lashes out, breaking Charles's jaw.

Afterwards, George recounts what he actually said to the trustees: Charles realises George was not responsible for the falsehood that got him imprisoned; it was someone else who invented the story. In a tearful reunion, they vow to never betray each other again.

Meanwhile, at Buckingham Palace, Prince Albert meets with the Allocations Board. There is a discrepancy between the Board's account of the show and what Charles Tipton said to him, and suspects George Tipton is trying to 'embarrass' him. After an investigation, he finds out it was Charles Tipton who spoke to him and not George. Moreover, he learns that Charles Tipton has been jailed for 'embarrassing' the monarch before: a serial offender! He sends a letter to Charles Tipton's trustees.

Unknown to George and Charles, two clauses were added to the Trust by the courtier: a) They must never discover their father; b) They must never embarrass the Monarch. There are rewards to the trustees for exposing an infringement, and the trustees agreed to take the reward for a minor charge. However this got heavily embellished by a local band of paid-for ragamuffin 'witnesses'. The trustees were remorseful about what happened but unable to do anything about it.

Meanwhile, in the theatre George grumbles about having to make a 'comedy' about workers, but as he progresses, remembers hundreds of drawings of workers he made as a child, in Tipton. The nature of the music-picture-show evolves into a portrayal of the back-breaking toil of the Black Country workers; also a celebration of them. Charles is very proud of this and the twins become closer. At the same time, Charles thinks of ongoing ideas to make a business out of George's animated picture technique. They form a business partnership. George decides he must take actual photographs of Tipton and the Black Country, and Charles go to book him a train ticket, but at a train station discovers there has been a major crash on the line, and books a stage coach instead. A Nordic-looking man observes this transaction.

Meanwhile, the trustees receive the letter from Prince Albert. They are morose about the bungle that happened seventeen years previously, and agree this job should be given to the professionals, as stated in the Trust; which is an elite unit of the Prussian Army based in Danzig. This unit have recently opened a branch office in London.

Meanwhile, in the theatre, Charles is organising a test performance with a working-class audience from south London to be held on Thursday 12th December, 1850, two hours before George's departure on the overnight stage coach to Tipton. George works like mad to prepare for the show and takes up residence in the theatre, along with his four-year-old son – George jnr.

The day of the show comes and there is frantic activity with dress rehearsals. The post arrives and Charles sees one post marked 'Birmingham'. Terrified he goes to a local workers café to read; the content is grim and he fears execution. He runs the mile-and-a-half to the Thames River and finds a steamer heading for America that evening. He books a working passage for himself, George and George Jnr. Next, he runs across Waterloo Bridge to buy a trunk On the way, he stops at the Somerset House registry office to find out who is father really is. Before he enters the office, his father breaks through – three-quarters ghost – and tells him, explaining the treachery that happened, and advises laying low in America until things blow over. Charles is stunned, buys a trunk, and transports it back to the theatre by horse and cart.

George is busy with preparing the show, so Charles packs all George's animated picture shows into the trunk. The audience arrives. The Nordic-looking man is amongst them. The show is a fantastic success. Once it ends, Charles hassles George and his son out the back onto the waiting horse and cart and races down to the river. Only then does Charles reveal what has happened. George is confused but wants to complete his show by taking the photos of the Black Country. Charles negotiates a passage for George on the next boat the following week.

Charles and George Jnr. undertake the gruelling Atlantic voyage and arrive eleven days later. On a railway platform in Philadelphia as wait for a train. Charles notices copies of the Birmingham Post unloading; and buys a copy. Here, he reads that George Tipton was killed just over a week ago, on Friday 13th December 1850, by highwaymen a few miles outside the Black Country. Charles is mortified, and tells young George his father has become a hero. The truth is more chilling than he imagined; Charles has the trunk locked up for a hundred-and-sixty years and vows to live a simple life, and never reveal his heritage.

Returning to present time:

Against Charlotte Tipton's advice, Georgina rummages through the trunk and discovers their true heritage. No sooner does this happen than George William manifests, and whisks them off to a fortress in Arizonan desert, claiming the feared "Devils from Danzig' are indeed on the way to kidnap them. Their magical adventure begins.

Book Two
'The Return'
(85,000 words approx.)

It is 2019. Having pitched for the best part of 200 years to run an immaculate world empire, George William is accepted, and back on Earth to accomplish this mission. He is joined by Aloysius Figgis - a direct descendant of the 19th C Horatio Figgis - plus the two Tipton girls, Georgina and Charlotte, who he abducted from their Pittsburgh home, saving them from the feared 'Devils from Danzig' - who were in hot pursuit.

Aloysius Figgis is a robot expert and has been working exclusively for George William for the past thirty years; in that time he has constructed hundreds of secret underground robot bases, populated by hundreds of millions of robots designed to implement George William's perfect world empire. There is a problem: Zakamonsky has turned up; Zakamonsky and his advanced army of two-hundred aliens who have been living in the old Teutonic sewers of Gdansk/Danzig for the last three-hundred years.

The lives of the Tipton girls are catapulted from ordinary suburban life in Pittsburgh into the bizarre magical world of George William and Figgis.

I am sorry, but that is all you are ging to learn about The Return for the moment. I intend to pitch a modified version of the story as a feature film. Best not to give away the secrets, just yet. I hope you understand.

www.dayfilm.com

Printed in Poland
by Amazon Fulfillment
Poland Sp. z o.o., Wrocław

76124033R00128